PURSUIT

US MARSHAL THRILLERS
BOOK 5

JODI BURNETT

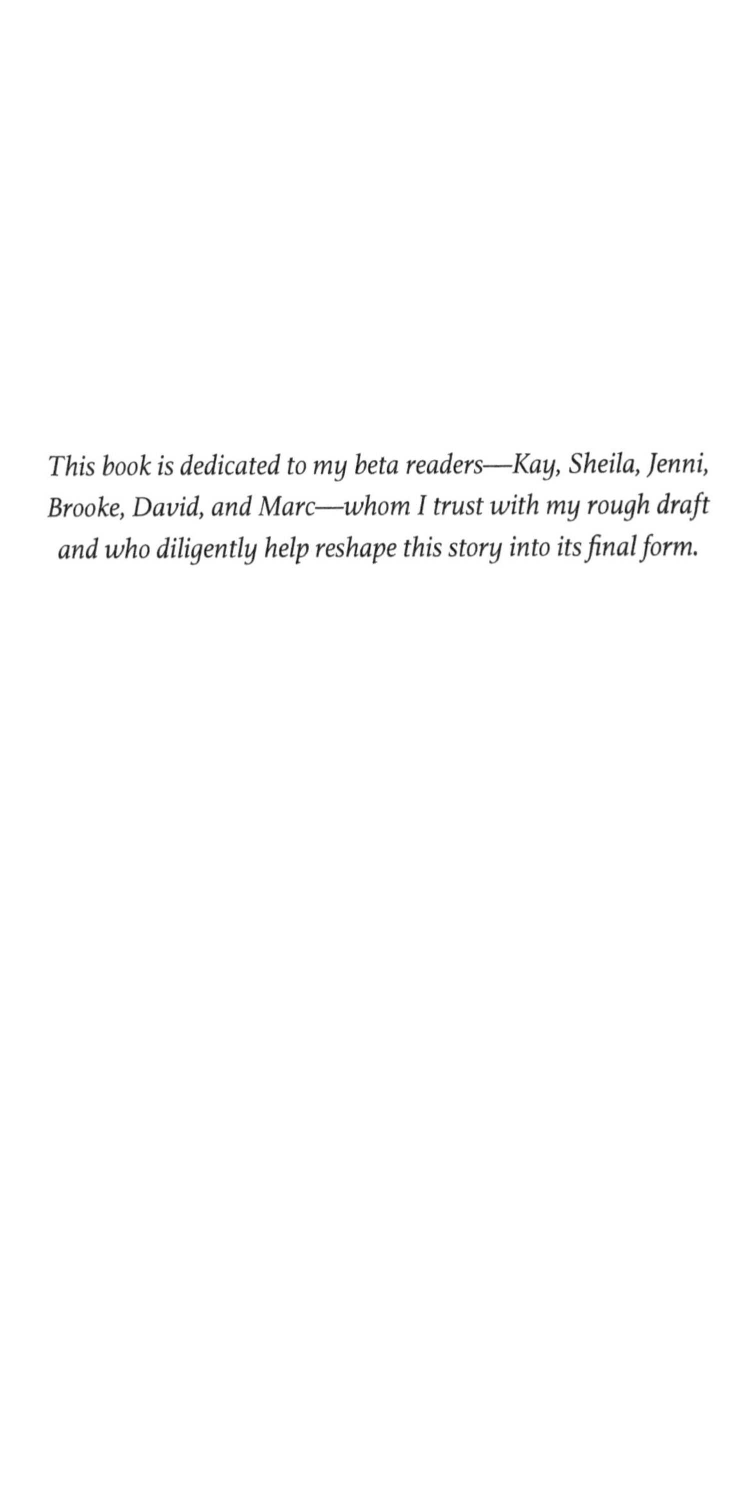

This book is dedicated to my beta readers—Kay, Sheila, Jenni, Brooke, David, and Marc—whom I trust with my rough draft and who diligently help reshape this story into its final form.

PURSUIT

PROLOGUE

Ian McCallum ran his hand through his dirty hair, sweeping it back before he replaced his ball cap. He ought to get a shower, not to mention a haircut, since the most recent photos of him show his shoulder-length mop. The beard was new, though, and helped to obscure his features. Adjusting his mirrored aviator sunglasses, he passed an IHOP. The smell of pancakes and bacon nearly drew him in, but he pressed on and crossed the street from the Goodwill shop to the Army/Navy Surplus store. He'd been in hiding for almost two months after his escape from FBI custody in Denver last June, but the feds were closing in. He had no time to waste.

Ian was ready to make his move and lean on his contact in Canada. But before he could do that, he had to prepare himself for crossing the rugged northern mountain country of Montana. He'd already resupplied his ammunition at a nearby sporting goods store, but he needed to spread out his other purchases so he'd be harder to track. The Goodwill outfitted him with clothing that blended in with the everyday people of Kalispell, Montana, and the local Surplus shop would provide the rest.

Ian crossed a mostly empty parking lot to the glass-fronted store with ARMY/NAVY in large red letters propped upright on the roof. On his way to the front doors, he passed a coin laundry and a marquee sign posted on the brick wall of the single-story building that said, "Fate whispers to the Warrior, 'You cannot withstand the storm.' The Warrior whispers back, 'I am the storm.'" The truth of that slogan was both more profound and far uglier than the author of the quote could have possibly imagined. A bitter grin spread across Ian's lips.

He studied his reflection and that of the surrounding area in the wall of plate-glass windows as he walked by a display of camp chairs in front of the store, making certain no one was following him. It was his habit to be on constant alert—twenty-four-seven. Seeing nobody, he ducked between the dual American flags posted on either side of the double doors. Clenching his jaw, he willfully ignored the faint, weathered stirring in his heart at the sight of Old Glory and entered the building.

There was an older man at the counter, obviously a vet by the look of the patches sewn onto his vest. His baseball cap confirmed; he had fought in Vietnam. Even after Ian's change in ideology, he still held great respect for the nation's warriors. The guy took in Ian's appearance and gave him a nod. "Morning." Military men recognized each other. It was something they easily sensed from one another's bearing. Or maybe it was the distinct haunting that hovered in their eyes.

Ian nodded back but said nothing. He scanned the hand-written signs hanging from the ceiling and walked toward the camping and survival section. He'd found sturdy black pants at the Goodwill earlier, but still required a good coat, a camouflage beanie and plenty of gear, including maps of the national park, for his long hike north to the border. Two more burner phones completed his shopping list.

It was time to locate a buyer for the top-secret information he had stolen, and he had to do it fast. Money was the sole thing he had to have in order to disappear forever, and it would take a serious amount. He had hoped to find a place to lie low so he could wait for the highest bidder, but the perimeter was closing in. With the feds on his trail, it was only a question of how long before they had him in custody once again. And the next time, he would be on his own. He'd already burned the single trump card he had with the FBI—the one get-out-of-jail-free pass. If they caught him a second time, he would spend the rest of his life in Leavenworth.

He had tried twice that morning to call his contact in Canada. Both of his calls were sent to voicemail. He left no messages and tossed the burner phone he'd used into the Whitefish River. His failure to reach the man who could broker the sale of state secrets was both frustrating and alarming. Was he discovered? If so, Ian was screwed.

He grabbed five MREs to bolster his survival meal options. The military Meals Ready to Eat provided valuable calories that would help him survive a long stretch in the wilderness. He would have to hide out in Glacier National Park until he could reach his contact and arrange both the sale of information and safe border passage. Secretly crossing into Canada used to be like taking a Sunday stroll. With the new administration, those days were over.

He carried his items to the counter, and the old vet rang them up. "Camping in the Park? It's a little late in the year."

Ian narrowed his gaze behind his mirrored glasses. He was suspicious of casual questions. In fact, he didn't believe in such a thing. "No. Just resupplying before the prices go up during hunting season."

"Not a bad idea." The clerk bagged his things and rang up the total. Ian paid in cash, thanked the man, and left.

He scanned the cars in the parking lot, searching for law enforcement lying in wait, but the vehicles were all empty. Absentmindedly, Ian wondered if he would ever stop watching for enemies, even when one day he was free, sitting on his own private beach most likely somewhere in the South Pacific. He doubted it. The specter of getting captured would always haunt him.

Crossing the lot, he made his way north up US Highway 2. He'd only walked about two blocks before a county sheriff's vehicle slowed beside him. The deputy rolled down his passenger-side window. "You new in town?" he hollered.

Ian's muscles tensed, preparing for a fight. He drew in a long, cool breath to calm his nerves. "Just passing through."

"Where ya headed?" The deputy gave him a long look before glancing at the road in front of him.

Knowing he had to give a location along the way but not wanting to divulge that his destination was Glacier, he answered, "I got a cousin up in Helena Flats."

"Really, that's where I'm from. Who's your cousin? I probably know him."

"*Her* name is Felicia Butler." He'd used the name of his first-grade teacher. It was better to use a real name than to make one up on the spot. When you tried that, your brain offered up names like John Smith or something equally unbelievable.

"Nope. Can't say I know any Felicias." The deputy kept pace with Ian as cars passed him in the left lane. "You planning on walking all the way up there?"

"Nah. She's headed down to pick me up, but I thought I'd meet her along the road. No use just sitting around." Ian's damp neck stuck to the collar of his shirt. Why was this guy asking him so many questions? Was he suspicious for some reason? The feds had probably posted his mugshot.

Ian's benefactor had shipped his long gun to a post office box less than half a mile away in Evergreen, the key to which was in his front pants pocket. But he couldn't retrieve the weapon with the deputy marking his every step. Ian mentally ran through the various weapons he had on himself. He carried a concealed pistol and two blades but hoped he wouldn't have to use any of them to dispatch the guy.

"Okay. I guess it won't help for me to offer you a ride, then."

"No, but thanks anyway."

The deputy watched him for several more paces, seemingly trying to make a decision. Finally, he bobbed his chin. "You have a nice day."

Ian raised his hand in a casual friendly wave, though his pulse raced and sweat trickled down his spine. He kept his eyes on the cruiser until it signaled left two blocks later, but he wouldn't breathe easy until he collected his M4 rifle and disappeared into the national park. As soon as the deputy was out of sight, Ian crossed a side street and turned right. He passed the Glacier Mercantile Center and followed back roads to the local post office.

Relief at finding his weapon waiting for him in the oversized postal box eased the tension in Ian's shoulders. He carried the package out of the building, dropping the mail key in the trash can by the door. All that remained to do that day was to hitch a ride north to West Glacier where he would reassemble his M4 and head north.

CHAPTER 1

Dirk slicked back his damp hair on his way out of the bedroom. He rolled up the sleeves on his shirt to mid-forearm before accepting the mug of coffee Emory offered him. Peering through the steam at the three kids perched on stools in front of the kitchen bar, he grinned. Somehow, this fivesome had become a family over the past nine months.

It had been a rocky time. After the Miller family, who had been in witness protection, was attacked, and the kids' father was killed, they discovered that their mother had paid to have him murdered. She was now in prison and would be long after her children grew into adulthood. The Miller kids had nowhere to go, unless social services separated them into three different foster homes. But Dirk had refused to allow that to happen. He couldn't bear the idea of them being torn apart, especially knowing that no foster family was prepared to deal with the potential danger looming from a Ukrainian mob family. He had made a knee-jerk decision to be the one who took them in. Emory had agreed to move in and help him. Shortly after that, he had proposed to her and now they were engaged, with a full-fledged family.

Kendall—fifteen for exactly six weeks and three more days—who informed him daily of the countdown until she was sixteen, was still socially tentative at school. She had been a popular cheerleader before her family entered WITSEC. Now she no longer liked to draw attention to herself. Jack, at fourteen, did his best to be the man of the household for his siblings. He put forth a brave front, but his mother's betrayal had crushed his heart. How would the kid ever get over his mom paying to have his dad killed? Then there was Joey, an adorable nine-year-old. He seemed the most well-adjusted of the three except for his constant concern that his brother and sister were okay. Dirk had grown to love the kids deeply. They, together with him and Emory, made a solid family.

"You kids about ready? The bus will be here in five minutes."

Kendall's eyes pleaded with him. "You know, if I had my driver's license, we wouldn't have to take the school bus. We could leave fifteen minutes later."

Emory slid a forest-green blazer on over her white silk blouse, pulling her long golden hair out from underneath the collar. "You're not even sixteen yet." She drained the last sip of joe from her mug.

"But I will be in October. That's only six weeks and three days away."

Dirk chuckled, remembering how much he had wanted the freedom of a license at her age. "We need to get you signed up for Driver's Ed. Check in with your school counselor about that."

"Can't you teach me?"

"We'll help you practice. But a formal class will teach you all the rules of driving. Plus, I think we get a break on car insurance if you complete one." Emory crossed the room and picked Joey's backpack up from the floor by the door. "Dirk, did you sign Joey's reading log?"

"Not yet. How long did you read last night, Joe?"

"An hour, I think. Yeah, actually an hour."

"Did not." Jack gave his little brother a gentle shove. "You were dead asleep by eight-thirty when I came in."

Joey smirked and pushed against his brother's shoulder. "Okay, so more like thirty minutes, I guess."

"Well," Dirk split open a banana from the fruit bowl. "Get your folder out so we can sign it."

Joey hopped down from his stool and grabbed the pack Emory held out. She grinned at Dirk, and he winked in response. Here they were, a full-fledged family. Mostly normal—other than the weekly therapy sessions the kids attended to help them deal with the trauma of violence ending in the loss of their parents the previous fall. They seemed to land fairly well... considering their lives had been torn apart, turned upside down, and inside out.

"Dirk," Emory broke through his musing. "Have you had a chance to swing by the bakery to taste the wedding cake flavor options?"

"You know, Em, I couldn't care less what kind of cake we have. Choose whatever you like—you and your mother, that is." He gave her a toothy smile to show that he was mostly teasing. In truth, he had hoped for a small, simple wedding with just Emory's family, the kids and a few close friends, but the plans were growing the more Emory and her mom talked. He didn't mind, though. He wanted Emory to have everything she dreamed of.

"I need your help. The ceremony is only a week away." An alarm sounded on Emory's phone. "Time to go, kiddos!" She tapped the screen to silence the sound.

The three kids moved toward the front door. Kendall and Joey hugged Dirk when they passed by. Jack bumped into his shoulder and tossed his chin. "See ya." Dirk clapped him on his back.

Emory hugged each kid as they left the house. "Have a good day!" She closed the door behind them and joined Dirk at the kitchen window to watch them until the bus came. "You know, I still worry about them when they leave in the mornings until we get home after work."

"The Kovalenko crime family has dispersed, and we haven't heard from or seen any action from their extended relatives in New York. I'm confident they would have struck by now if they had intended to." Dirk assured her.

"Probably. But how will we ever be able to fully let our guard down?"

"I don't know. I suppose parents always worry, don't they?" They watched the kids climb up the steps into the yellow bus, and when the door closed, they turned to finish getting themselves ready to go. "Should we both drive today? I promised I'd stop by and see Caleb after work."

"Why don't you invite Laurie and Caleb for dinner

tonight, instead? Joey would love it, and that way you won't have to give up time with the... with our... I don't know how to refer to them. I feel like they are our kids, but they're not. Not really. We won't ever be able to adopt them unless their mother agrees to it."

The Miller kids' mom was in prison for conspiracy to commit murder, which meant the kids needed foster care, but adoption was another thing. "It doesn't matter, does it? They are ours in all the ways that count. We love them like they are, and they love us too."

"You're right." Emory slid her arms around his waist and tilted her chin up to smile at him.

He bent to kiss her. "It's crazy, though, isn't it? I can't believe how we've become a true family over the past months."

"I think the intense way you saved their lives and have protected them since then has built immediate and ironclad bonds of trust between you all."

"You, too. You were there every minute and have been their rock through the rough emotional times."

She pressed her cheek against his chest and his arms enfolded her. "They've been through hell, that's for sure."

Dirk's memory skipped through scenes of the gunfight, blood, and death the kids experienced. They watched their dad get shot point blank in front of them. They faced a horrific terror, and then they learned that their mother had paid for their father's murder. It was overwhelming. He was proud of how well they were adjusting after all they'd been through.

Emory had jumped right in on his impulsive idea to give the kids a safe foster home so that they could stay together. He'd wanted to marry Em immediately, but Elaine Grey had bigger plans for her daughter's nuptials. Dirk kissed the top of Emory's head. "We'd better get going. The boss can be a real bear if I'm late to work."

"Yeah, yeah." She pushed away from him. "I've heard she's a tough cookie." Emory pulled hamburger meat from the freezer to defrost before she slipped on her pumps and slung the straps of her purse and computer bag over her shoulder. "Have you heard anything from Henry this past weekend?"

"No. His mom is visiting."

"I'm sure she's a tremendous help with the baby."

"Yeah, I think she'll be here for a few more days. Which is good. Hank could use a break."

"He's a great dad."

"He is. But he's running on all cylinders. He's going to have to find a balance before he runs himself into the ground."

Emory nodded thoughtfully. "Any word about Amy? How she's doing?"

"Hank hasn't said, and I don't ask. He'll tell me if he wants me to know."

"Men." Emory laughed and rolled her eyes. "Hey, if we're having Laurie and Caleb for dinner, we may as well invite Teresa, Tomas, and Henry's clan over. We can do something simple like sloppy joes or tacos."

Dirk chuckled and shook his head. Nothing was ever simple with Emory.

CHAPTER 2

Dirk and Emory drove into Billings together in his black Rubicon. Over the past several months, they'd both had to make compromises. Emory, wanting to see the kids off in the morning, had agreed to go to the office later than her usual routine, but for Dirk it was the opposite. He was up in time to say goodbye to Kendall, Jack, and Joey and then, it was out the door forty-five minutes before he was used to. This was one of the many changes they had faced becoming an instant family, and honestly one of the easier adjustments.

Lack of privacy was new to Dirk, and he didn't exactly love that particular change. Time with Emory alone was a commodity. Getting up a little earlier meant they had the drive-time to the office together without interruption. But it was also a transition period from family mode to their professional mindsets, so unless there was a pressing matter at home, they tended to focus on work.

When they arrived at the office, Emory turned left

and went into her inner sanctum—where she could close the door when she needed space. Dirk peeled off to the right, tossing his jacket on the back of his desk chair before treading to the breakroom to start the coffee. If he were lucky, Teresa had already brewed a pot, but he saw that wasn't the case that morning.

Teresa and Hank arrived just before 9:00 am. Their desks faced each other on the opposite wall from Dirk's, and all three of them gathered at Hank's workstation to view his most recent photos of Hank's new daughter, Evelyn—Evie for short—who had just turned five months old.

"Here, she's laughing and babbling. I'm pretty sure she said, 'Da-da!'." Hank swiped to the next image. "Look, she's waving at me in this one."

Teresa winked at Dirk over the top of Hank's head, and he chuckled quietly in response. "She's a cute kid, Hank. Hey, Emory wants to have you all over for sloppy joes tonight. Can you come?"

"You bet. Any night I don't have to cook is a yes from me. Tomas and I will be there. I can bring something for dessert." Teresa straightened and stretched her back.

Dirk nudged his partner. "How about you, Hank? Everyone would love to see Evie, and your mom is welcome unless she'd rather have a break."

Hank gave a short laugh. "I doubt I could pry Evie out of her arms that long, but I'm sure she'd like to come."

"Good. I'll let the boss know."

"Let me know what?" Emory came out of her office carrying her laptop and a cup of tea. "Monday morning meeting in..." she glanced at her watch, "five minutes."

"Everyone can come to dinner."

"Great." She offered them a brief smile. "Now let's get to work."

Dirk gave her a mock salute and went to refill his coffee before following his co-workers into the conference room.

"I was just notified of a manhunt for a fugitive named Ian McCallum. He's an ex-special forces operator gone bad. Ian McCallum had been an Army Ranger until 2023, when he received a dishonorable discharge. After that, he sold himself to the Devil, becoming a contract killer for hire. Blackmailing government and military officials provided him with a lucrative second income before the FBI captured and arrested him. Apparently, by leaning hard on several of his blackmail victims in high levels of the government, McCallum came into possession of some top-secret military secrets that, if given to the wrong world players, would put our nation's security at risk.

Dirk leaned forward, bracing his forearms against the conference table. "Did the FBI secure that information when they apprehended him?"

"No. They found no such evidence and worse, McCallum escaped FBI custody two months ago. I just got off the phone with Reagan, the special agent in charge at the Billings office. They've found evidence that McCallum's in Montana and suspect he'll be heading up through Montana toward the Canadian border, and they are putting together a joint task force to track and find him before he can reach his Canadian contact with the stolen military information." Emory pressed several keys on her laptop before turning the screen to face them.

"This is McCallum's official Army photo and his recent mugshot."

Dirk's gut stirred with acid as he studied the images. One was of a clean-cut second lieutenant. The second was that of a longish-haired, unshaven Captain in the Army Rangers. It was the ultimate betrayal to sell out one's brothers-in-arms to the highest bidder. Guys like McCallum made Dirk sick. "Why was he pushed out of the Army?"

"He attempted to sell secret information to an undercover CIA agent." Emory's green eyes met his. "The FBI wants me to send you and Henry to join the task force." She never used the shortened version of Flannigan's first name, whom the rest of the world called Hank.

Dirk's nervous system hummed with ire. His immediate internal reaction was to yell, "Let's go!" But he had a family to think about now, and he hesitated. This was a new sensation for him. They had had no cases involving travel since the Miller kids moved in with them.

Hank's cheeks grew ruddy, and he cleared his throat. "I can't go on the road right now. My mom leaves the day after tomorrow, and I don't have anyone to care for Evelyn. I'm sorry. I know I have to get something worked out."

Emory's gaze settled on Hank. "Could you ask your mother to stay a little longer?"

"I would, but she's speaking at a conference."

"And Amy?"

"She's still too unstable."

Emory bit down on her lower lip and again looked at Dirk. "It looks like you'll be the lone deputy marshal from our office. I know they want you specifically because of your knowledge of the wilds of northern Montana and your tracking skills. SAC Reagan expects you at their briefing with Homeland and the USMS SOG this afternoon at one o'clock."

Dirk drew in a long breath and let it go along with his apprehension about leaving his family. "Will do. After this meeting, I'll go home and pack. Good to know the Special Operations Group will be involved."

Hank rapped his knuckles on the table. "Sorry, I can't go with you. But I promise full back up from the office."

"You'll be where you're most needed. Did you ever talk with Laurie Dillenger about watching Evie in situations like this? She works from home and would probably appreciate making a few extra dollars now and then."

"Yeah..." Hank deflated into his chair.

Teresa grinned at him. "It's hard to leave your baby. Believe me, I get it. But it gets easier, especially if you have someone you can truly trust to watch her."

"I know. I'll talk to Laurie. Maybe I can start off with just a few hours though."

Emory closed her laptop. "You can speak with her tonight. She and Caleb are coming to dinner, too. I know there are extenuating circumstances, Henry, but you need to work out your childcare if you want to continue in your position."

"Yes, ma'am. I'll talk to her."

"Good. Dirk, keep me posted regarding working together with the FBI. I don't imagine you'll be home for our dinner tonight."

"Probably not. We'll want to strike while his trail is still hot."

As they all filed out of the meeting room, Teresa asked Emory, "How are the wedding plans coming? Will Dirk be back in time for the ceremony? It's just next weekend."

"They'd better find McCallum before then. If not, he'll permanently be in the wind with plenty of opportunity to sell those precious military secrets. And I have no doubt he'll have bidders tripping over themselves to buy whatever it is he has." She sighed, and her gaze zeroed in on Dirk. "I'm going on the assumption you'll be home by Saturday, but if not, work comes first. We can reschedule."

Dirk bobbed his head, hoping he wouldn't have to let Emory down. Rescheduling sounded much easier than it would be, both emotionally and in practice. "We'll find him."

CHAPTER 3

Emory returned to her office with a heavy heart. Work had to come first, but she'd be lying if she said she wasn't worried about their wedding. Everything was ready. She had ordered the musicians, cake, and flowers. Both Kendall's and her dress had been through their final fittings, the boys had reserved matching tuxedos, and her mother had worked tirelessly, attending to all the little details that made such a day so special. Emory murmured a quiet prayer that God would not only protect the task force, but allow them to catch McCallum before Friday.

"Hey, Chief," Teresa's voice startled Emory from her worries. "You okay?"

"Yes. Yes, of course." Emory touched her heated cheeks with cool fingers.

"Don't worry. If anyone can wrangle McCallum in, it's Sterling."

"I know. I'm just trying to run some contingency plans through my mind in case he doesn't catch him before this weekend. I guess I should let everyone know it's a possibility that we might have to postpone."

Teresa crossed her arms and leaned against the office doorjamb. "I wouldn't. At least not until Thursday. That would give everybody plenty of time to adjust their plans."

"But what about the musicians and the cake?"

"Hopefully, they'll be flexible. It's not like September is a huge wedding month in Montana."

Emory dropped into her chair, struggling between being the professional she was and a woman dreaming of her wedding day. "I suppose."

"Either way, Laurie and I still plan to take you out for a bachelorette party. We're making Hank watch all the kids since Dirk will be on the job."

"You know I don't want to do anything wild."

"I know, I know." Teresa laughed. "Don't worry. We are thinking of dinner and drinks. That's all, but just us girls."

"Good." Emory took a deep breath and sat straighter in her chair. Time to get back to work. "Will you please let Henry know I'd like to see him?"

Teresa pushed herself off the door frame and called over her shoulder, "Hank, Chief wants to see you."

HANK GLANCED at Dirk to see if he knew why the chief had summoned him to her office, but his partner shrugged and continued reading the most recent FBI brief on McCallum. It was rare for his boss to call him into her private space, so he was mildly apprehensive.

"Yeah, boss?"

"Henry, come in. Shut the door and have a seat."

His concern ratcheted up a notch, and his gut squirmed. Was he in trouble? She was probably pissed that he hadn't arranged for overnight childcare by now. Evie was already five months old.

Hank did as the chief asked and slid into one of the two chairs before her desk. "What's up?"

"I wanted to check in with you to see how things are going. I know you filed a Parent Responsibility Case against Amy with the court when she refused to take her bipolar medication after Evie was born."

"Yeah, the PRE—the parent responsibility evaluation—was pricey but worth every penny if it helps keep Evelyn safe. That day I stopped by Amy's with formula and diapers and found Evie home alone, crying in her crib and Amy gone to the store, tipped the scales." Hank's mind shot back to the day he had discovered his tiny baby girl screaming from her bed. He had no idea how long Amy had left her by herself with no one to hear her. He breathed through a sudden rush of anger. "I have full custody until Amy earns back her privileges. *If* she does. They've given her six months to get her act together. She has another evaluation next month, but I don't think she's taking her meds still, so..."

"So, we can assume that you will carry on in the role of a single parent. Teresa is in the same boat, but she has transitioned from active deputy to primarily our office admin. However, we need only one of those in a workspace this size. I guess what I'm asking is if you want to continue on as a deputy marshal in this office?"

A chill washed through him, and he sat forward. "Of course I do. I know I've been preoccupied, Chief, and I'm sorry. But I love this job. I just need to work a few things out."

"Okay. Good. I'm relieved to hear it."

"Finding overnight care is a little tricky. Since I have the PRE preventing Amy's parental time, I also have to mind all *my* p's and q's. I'll ask Laurie if she can be on call for twenty-four-hour care when necessary, but she'll have to be a certified childcare giver before the court will approve. And Evie already spends all day at the daycare center unless my mom is visiting."

"Fine. I expect you to get that organized soon. It's been five months."

Air escaped from Hank's lungs, and he deflated in the chair. "I know. It's just that..."

"You hate the idea of leaving her. I understand. I really do. But this is your job, Henry. You need to decide if it's worth the time you spend away from home."

"It is. It's just not how I figured things would be, you know? I always wanted a family with a dad *and* a mom. It would be so much easier to leave if I knew Evie was with a loving mother while I was gone."

"Well, maybe Amy will get the help she needs. Until then, let me know if there is anything we can do to support you."

"Thanks, Chief. I won't let you down again." Hank returned to his desk feeling slightly nauseous. "Hey, T, do you have Laurie Dillenger's phone number?"

CHAPTER 4

irk felt for the kid. Hank had always loved being on the road for the job. It was one of the major issues that stood between him and his ex-wife. When Amy got pregnant and subsequently diagnosed with bipolar disorder, Hank's life took a sharp left turn. It was a high-risk pregnancy, and the situation worsened when Amy refused to take her medication. Their concurrent divorce gutted Hank, and now he had to deal with the pressures of his job and being a single parent.

"Hey, Kid. Don't worry about it. You'll get it all figured out."

"I hope I do before I lose my job."

"You're not going to get fired. Besides, I'm sure Laurie will be happy to help you out."

"Let's hope." Hank took the number from Teresa and turned toward his desk to make the call.

Dirk went back to the FBI briefs and made a call of his own. "Special Agent Reagan, please. This is Dirk Sterling with the Marshals Office."

After a minute, a voice barked over the phone, "Sterling, where are you? I want you to be here for these briefings. The next one is at two o'clock."

"Yes, sir." Dirk checked his watch and swore under his breath. "I'll be there." It was already almost noon, and he still had to get home and pack. "I just want to make sure your office has my partner's contact information. He'll be supporting me from here." The SAC passed him off to his admin, and Dirk confirmed that Hank would have all the information he needed from the FBI.

He shut down his computer and grabbed his jacket. "See you guys this weekend," he said to Hank and Teresa. Hank raised a hand in farewell, turning back to his phone call.

"Hope so." Teresa's black eyebrows raised in circumspection.

Ignoring her doubt, Dirk stepped into Emory's office, closing the door behind him. "I'm out."

Emory came around her desk to embrace him. Her hair smelled like lilacs, and he pulled her closer so he could bury his nose in her blonde waves. "I'll be gone before the kids get home from school. I won't get to say goodbye to them."

"I'll explain. They'll understand."

"I guess. The only thing that makes leaving worthwhile is the idea of bringing this traitor to justice. There's nothing worse than a soldier betraying his brothers-in-arms. It's one thing to become a mercenary, but selling out the guys you fought shoulder-to-shoulder with is unforgivable."

"It's lousy, that's for sure. So, go find him. And do it

before Saturday." Emory smiled up at him, and he bent to kiss her goodbye.

"I'll do the best I can. But..."

She pressed her index finger against his lips. "Focus on the job at hand and stay safe. Don't be distracted. We're flexible on this end. Okay?"

"Okay." He kissed her again, hoping to convey his love and his disappointment at not being there with her the week before their wedding, or worse, on their wedding day.

"Everything will work out, Dirk. You zero in on the job."

Emory walked him to the elevator. She blew him a kiss as the compartment doors closed between them. When he could no longer see her, Dirk's focus shifted entirely to the task at hand, and he rushed home to pack his bag. He packed two handguns and his Marshal-issue M4 Carbine. Pulling out his ammo container, he checked to be sure it was full. Cold-weather gear was next on the list. He packed the clothes he needed along with his body armor and went to the garage to gather his sub-zero camping gear, just in case.

Dirk made a thick roast beef sandwich with extra mayonnaise, filled a baggie with potato chips and took an apple for lunch in the car. He scrounged through the kitchen drawers to find some paper to write a note for the kids, and he left it on the counter. Next, he wrote a private message to his bride-to-be, slid it inside an envelope, sealed it and placed it on her pillow. His chest felt heavy as he lifted his weapons and his pack. He was already missing his new family.

Dirk locked the door behind him and headed out to his car. Thunder rumbled overhead, and icy sleet dropped like tiny frozen spears from the sky. He ran to his Rubicon before the sky opened up. He put his supplies in the back and darted to the driver's door. Once inside, he sighed. Frigid rain in Billings meant freezing snow up north. It was early for snowfall in Billings, but he knew it was common to get a couple of feet of the white stuff closer to the Canadian border this time of year.

His phone rang from the dashboard. "Sterling, here."

Hank's voice echoed through the speakers. "Hey, Dirk. Reagan from the FBI office just called. He wants you to meet everyone at the FBI field office in Bozeman. All the agencies on the task force are gathering together there, and he'll brief everyone at one time. The new meeting time is four o'clock."

"Got it. Glad you caught me before I drove back into Billings. I'll head to Bozeman now, but it's a two-hour drive. Will you let him know?"

"No problem. Nice of him to ask if you wanted a ride on the chopper." Hank said sarcastically.

Dirk chuffed. "I'd rather drive myself, anyway. That way I have my own car out there." He turned on the defrost and windshield wipers to keep the sleet from freezing to the glass as he turned west toward the ramp onto I-90. He found a country music channel on the radio and settled in for the two-hour drive. Hoping the weather would clear soon and that not too much snow would fall, he sank his teeth into his beefy sandwich and hummed along to the western song.

CHAPTER 5

Teresa offered to drive Emory home since she had ridden with Dirk that morning and he had to take his car. And since the entire crew was meeting at Dirk's house for sloppy joes, it worked out. They had to stop by the elementary school to pick up Teresa's son, Tomas, from after-school care, and then they drove to the outskirts of the city where Dirk's farmhouse was.

Teresa turned onto the gravel road that led to Sterling's place. The white house had black shutters and a deep front porch the length of the house where rocking chairs and a porch swing waited for a long conversation. Light from the front porch and windows welcomed them as they pulled into the drive. "You're lucky that Kendall's old enough to babysit Joey. I'm sure she's way more flexible than the teachers at the school's setup."

"It is nice, but she gets equally grouchy if I'm late." Emory laughed, enjoying the connection she and Teresa made as working moms. "Come on, Tomas. I bet Joey is dying to play with you."

The front door burst open, and Joey darted out, launching himself off the porch, missing the steps entirely. "Tomas! Let's build a fort. Dirk has some extra boards he said we could use." Tomas shoved his backpack onto the floor of his mom's car and took off after Joey toward the large outbuilding that Dirk used as a workshop and storage space on the acreage behind the house.

Emory and Teresa went inside. "Can I pour you a glass of wine?"

Teresa slid onto a bar stool at the kitchen counter. "Yes, please. That sounds perfect. What can I do to help get dinner started?"

"Nothing, right now." Emory glanced at the clock on the oven. "We still have a few minutes to just relax."

She uncorked a bottle of Cabernet and took two long-stemmed glasses from the cupboard. Kendall sat spread out on the living room sofa watching TV and scrolling on her phone. They had recently given her permission to open private profiles on Instagram and Snapchat under strict rules that she only friend people she met in person from school. She continued to be forbidden from contacting friends from her old life and from accepting any communication from people she didn't know directly from her new identity.

"How was school, Kendall?" Emory poured the wine.

"Fine."

Ugh. As soon as the question left Emory's lips, she remembered not to ask banal questions that would get one-word answers, or that was exactly what she would get in response. "Didn't you have a quiz in science today? Tell me about it."

Kendall rested her phone in her lap and twisted around to face Emory. "It sucked. I thought I was ready, but I only knew about half the answers." She rested her chin on the back of the couch with a frown.

"I know you studied. What do you think happened?"

"I think I studied the wrong chapter." Kendall's phone dinged, and she flopped back around to read the message.

Emory and Teresa shared a knowing look. Teresa sipped her wine. "Where's Jack?"

"Football practice. He should be home any minute. We carpool with a couple of the other parents. It's looking like he might get the chance to play quarterback this year on the junior varsity team."

"That's awesome. Hopefully, that helps him adjust. I know he misses pitching."

Emory glanced at Kendall to see if she was listening. Emory and Dirk tried not to bring up the kids' past if they could help it. But luckily Kendall was engrossed in her text conversation and not paying any attention to the women in the kitchen.

She lowered her voice. "Yeah, he's a natural athlete, so he is good at whatever he tries, but his first love is baseball. We're assessing the risk. So far, there have been no attempts from anyone related to the Kovalenko family to contact the kids. If that continues, Dirk might agree to let Jack try out for baseball in the spring."

"Have you told him?"

"No. We'd hate for him to be disappointed if he can't."

"Makes sense." Teresa reached for the bottle to refill her glass.

Emory poured a little olive oil in a large cast-iron Dutch oven and turned on the gas flame on the stove beneath it. She opened the fridge and pulled out the defrosted hamburger meat and placed it in the pot, stirring it until it browned. "Hank said he and Evie will be here at 6:30. Did you ever hear from Laurie?"

"No, I think Hank talked to her."

"We'll have plenty either way." Emory poured the sloppy joe mix into the cooked meat and set it to simmer. She was placing buns in a basket when the front door swung open and Jack tromped in wearing a mud-smeared football uniform and carrying his helmet and pads.

"Hey," he greeted Emory and Teresa. He raised his chin to acknowledge his sister, who responded with a 'hey' of her own. "What's for dinner? It smells good, and I'm starving."

"Sloppy joes. They'll be ready by the time you get out of the shower." Emory smirked. "You seem extra dirty tonight."

"Coach made us play through the rain. It was freezing!" His eyes sparkled, and he grinned. "I need a snack before my shower though; my stomach feels like it's turning inside out." Jack dropped his filthy gear by the door and went to open the refrigerator. He stood staring at the contents. Reaching inside, he came out with bread, sliced ham, cheese, and the jar of mayonnaise.

The women watched him make a double-decker

sandwich for his pre-shower nosh. He took a ladened plate into his bedroom, and Teresa raised her eyebrows at Emory. "That's his snack?"

"You would never believe how hungry that boy is. All. The. Time. Watch, he'll eat all that and at least three sloppy joes with all the sides for dinner. Dirk says he remembers being hungry all the time when he was that age, too. I guess Jack's growing."

"I guess I'd better prepare myself. Tomas will be that age before I know it."

At 6:40, Henry knocked and opened the front door. He carried Evie in her car seat, and Laurie and her son Caleb followed him in.

"Welcome! Laurie, I'm glad you could make it. I'm sure Henry told you that Dirk was called out for work."

"Yes, like usual, right? Thanks for inviting us."

"Sure. Hey Caleb, Joey and Tomas are out in the workshop. Would you mind going to tell them that dinner is ready?"

By the time everyone had assembled, Emory had finished setting out the food. She stood back, waiting for her guests and the kids to serve themselves. Kendall and all the boys sat in front of the TV while they ate, watching one of the Marvel movies, while the adults sat at the dining room table.

Henry rocked Evie's chair and smiled at his little girl. "Laurie has agreed to watch Evie for me if I have to be out-of-town overnight."

Emory smiled at the pretty brunette. "That's great, Laurie."

"Yeah, but I have to become a certified caregiver to

check the right box for the custody judge. I'm not sure what all that involves or how long it will take, but I'm happy to help. And honestly, I can use the extra income while I'm building up my graphic design business."

Henry swung his gaze to Emory. "My mom had to leave today, and I don't have anyone else who can watch Evie overnight, so I can't join Dirk in the field yet. But as soon as Laurie is ready, I'll catch up to him." He turned to Laurie. "I looked into the requirements and for watching one child, you need a 15-hour pre-licensing training which includes CPR/First Aid training, and a medication administration course. So, it shouldn't take too long."

Emory sighed. "Hopefully, Dirk will be home before then."

Laurie's eyes widened. "Oh, your wedding! That's supposed to be this weekend."

"Yes, well, we'll see." Emory shrugged, hoping she looked flexible though her heart ached with the possibility of having to postpone.

Kendall stood amid the boys and slowly turned to face Emory. Her face was pale, and she held up her phone.

"What is it, Kendall? Is everything alright?" A lead ball dropped into Emory's stomach, and she pressed her palm against her queasy belly. "What's the matter?"

Kendall thrust her phone in Emory's direction. She hurried to her foster daughter's side to see what had upset her. Since she and Dirk took the Miller kids into their home, they'd become familiar with the social media platforms they allowed Kendall and Jack to use.

The page open on the phone was from Snapchat,

where a stream of icons next to the nonsensical chatter of teens filled the screen. Emory quickly scanned the text but saw nothing unusual. She looked to Kendall for an explanation.

"Look closer. See underneath this profile, it says 'by mention'? That means that this person added me as a contact through a tagged photo on someone else's post."

"Okay. Do you know who this is?" The icon was a cartoon version of a brown-haired boy with the username Fletch.

"I don't know. I mean, my boyfriend in Connecticut was Fletcher. Could it be him? Do you think he's found me and is trying to reach me?" Kendall's eyes held unbearable hope, but it was mixed with hard-earned fear. A fear Emory shared.

"I don't know, Kendall, but you cannot respond to this profile. Even if it is Fletcher. It isn't safe. I'll take this to Tech in the morning and see what they can discover. Let me have your phone."

Kendall hesitated. Emory understood, A teenage girl's entire life was on her phone, but this was not an ordinary girl.

"I'll return it to you as soon as possible, Kendall, but my first priority is the safety of you and your brothers."

Kendall's voice croaked from her throat. "Do you think they'll try to attack us—again?"

CHAPTER 6

Two hours after he left Billings, Dirk exited I-90 and drove to the FBI field office in Bozeman. The building complex where it was located looked more like stylish apartments, rather than the cement, no-frills federal buildings he was used to. He joined SAC Reagan in a room that smelled of overheated computers and K9s. Various law enforcement officers and agents filled the space. Representatives from the FBI, Homeland, USMS SOG, and even Forest Rangers had come together to be a part of the joint task force searching for Ian McCallum.

Dirk approached Reagan, who stood at the front of the room. "Agent Reagan, I'm Dirk Sterling." He held out his hand to shake Reagan's.

"*Special Agent in Charge* Reagan." The agent corrected as he pumped Dirk's hand. "Glad to see you made it. Find a seat, we'll be getting started soon."

Dirk did his best to keep his expression neutral in the face of his turgid, and thankfully temporary, boss as he moved to the back of the room to find a place to sit. He took a chair next to a Montana Forest Ranger, whose dark green campaign hat rested on the table in front of him.

"Always liked those Smokey Bear covers." Dirk held out his hand and introduced himself before he sat.

"It's the Montana pinch that makes 'em so sexy." The brown-haired Ranger's eyes sparked with mischief as he shook Dirk's hand. "Dan Lowry."

"Good to meet you, Dan. Ever worked with the FBI before?"

"On occasion. Done a few jobs with the Marshals, too. Mostly tracking fugitives, kind of like in this case."

"Most fugitives don't have the survival experience McCallum has. He'll be harder to find than most."

SAC Reagan cleared his throat and raised his voice. "Come to order, please. We are here to plan the search for Ian McCallum; ex-Special Forces operator and escaped FBI felon. McCallum escaped federal custody two days ago and is on the run. Not only is he an escaped convict, but he has access to top-secret military information that could jeopardize the security of our nation and the lives of hundreds of military personnel."

Two images appeared on a whiteboard at the front of the room. One was of a young, clean-cut McCallum as a second lieutenant in the Army. The other photo was of a unit wearing desert fatigues, presumably somewhere in the Middle East. Red ink circled the head of a man with longish dark hair and camo paint smeared across his face. It was hard to see the resemblance between the two photos, but it was there in his eyes.

Reagan read from his notes. "McCallum was in Delta

Force and was the lone survivor after his unit went out on a routine FID—Foreign Internal Defense mission—and their transport got hit with an IED. He blamed the Army for his loss, and when they dragged their heels on the investigation, McCallum became a problem child. They caught him trying to sell information to an undercover CIA officer and he received a dishonorable discharge for his efforts. When he got out, McCallum hired himself out as a mercenary and eventually an assassin.

"There are task forces like this one in each state along the northern border, but we believe he will most likely attempt a crossing somewhere in the wilderness between Minnesota and Washington. This group is responsible for covering the area from Yellowstone National Park up to and across the Montana/Canadian border. Our intel strongly suggests he is currently hiding out in Yellowstone, though he could have moved up into Missoula. McCallum is an expert survivalist. He can lie low for an indefinite amount of time and make his move when it suits him. We must find him before then." Reagan passed out printed sheets with the most recent photos of McCallum along with his height, weight, and other statistics.

Dirk took a page and handed the stack to Dan. "Spend any time in the military?"

Dan shook his head. "Nope. But I run across lots of men in the forest who have. Guys with McCallum's experience who don't seem to fit into regular society anymore."

Dirk nodded, considering the Ranger. "Do you agree

with Reagan that McCallum is hiding out in Yellowstone or Missoula?"

Dan studied him in return and finally must have decided to trust him with an honest answer. "Nope. I doubt a guy like this would bother hiding in a city. He's probably much closer to the border by now, if not already across it. Why would he wait?"

"That's what I'm thinking too. If it were me, I'd get out of Dodge as fast as I could. He has no motive to hang around and millions of green-backed reasons to bolt."

Reagan's voice interrupted their conversation. "SOG K9, divide yourselves among the teams. One dog per unit should do." Law enforcement officers shifted and merged until there were four groups. Three teams with dogs and a mix of two to three FBI, Marshals and Homeland Security agents. Dan slowly unfolded himself from his chair, surprising Dirk with his height. The Ranger had to be at least six-foot-five and wiry—probably not weighing more than one-eighty.

Together, he and Dirk made up the fourth team. The only one without K9 assistance. Dirk wished his friend Caitlyn Reed was there with her dog, Renegade, but she was currently out on family leave. It had been on his recommendation that Caitlyn had become a deputy US marshal. They'd worked several cases together, but before long she was on the fast track to success and had joined the Marshal's Special Operations Group. Caitlyn was like a little sister to him, and he couldn't be more proud of her.

"Looks like it's just the two of us," Dirk murmured.

"Works for me. Two men move through the mountains faster and quieter than three or four, and besides, you and I can start our search up north. I'm stationed up in Glacier and know the park like I know my face. If I were as smart as McCallum seems to be, that's where I'd head. Not just anyone could follow him through that terrain."

Dirk agreed that a smaller team would be more efficient. In fact, he would rather be on his own since he couldn't partner with either Hank or Caitlyn. He had no way of knowing what kind of skills Ranger Lowry had, or if he could count on him in a life-and-death situation.

Dirk drew a deep breath. "Okay. But before we head north, let's see if we can find any evidence that's where he is." Dirk pulled out his phone. "I'll send all this info to my partner in Billings. He'll be able to do some searching for us from there. I don't want to waste any time. I'm supposed to be getting married this coming weekend."

"You're kidding. I hope your girl is an understanding one. We'll be lucky if we catch McCallum by then."

"She gets it. In fact, she's my boss, so technically my being here was her decision." Dirk's phone buzzed. It was Emory. "Speak of the devil." He clicked on the call. "Hey Em, what's up?"

"Dirk! Thank heaven I caught you while you still have coverage."

His belly clamped down on a swirl of nerves. "What's wrong?"

"Someone Kendall doesn't know tried to contact her on Snapchat. The name of the profile is 'Fletch'. She's hoping it's her old boyfriend from Connecticut, but I explained she must not respond to him, even if it is. I took her phone and will give it to Tech in the morning to see what they can find, but I'm nervous."

"I'll come home. I don't want to take any chances. If I leave now, I can be home in two hours."

"No, stay there. The job you're on is crucial to national security. I can handle this."

"But I want to be there to protect you and the kids."

"I know. But remember, I'm also a deputy marshal, and I'm able to keep them safe. Plus, I have Henry and Teresa for backup if I need any. I didn't mean to worry you, but I knew you'd want to know. It's probably nothing, but I'd rather err on the side of caution."

Dirk ground his teeth together and resisted his instinct to rush home to protect his family. "Keep me posted. I'll have phone coverage for at least another day. I need Hank to do some searching for us before we go dark."

CHAPTER 7

Light infiltrated Ian's eyelids, but he kept them closed. His other senses searched the space around him on high alert. He heard nothing. Breathing in through his nose, he detected no scent other than the dank smell of the room. He sensed no unusual stimuli. Detecting no threat, he gradually opened his eyes.

Oh, yeah—he was on the lumpy, questionably clean bed in an out-of-the way, mostly empty, pay-by-the-hour motel outside of West Glacier, Montana. Cotton filled his skull, effects from downing most of the bottle of single malt scotch he had cuddled up to the night before. His mouth tasted like garbage.

His head throbbed when he swung his feet to the floor. Putting his faith in the hair-of-the-dog, he reached for what remained in the cloudy glass by his bed and downed it, immediately drawing in a sharp breath through his teeth against its bite. He tapped a cigarette out of the pack on the nightstand not hesitating to light it since he had disabled the smoke detector the night before. He sucked in the nicotine waiting for his mind to clear enough to get dressed.

Eventually, he plodded across the filthy carpet, not bothering to avoid the stains made from things he'd rather not think about, and turned on the shower. Lukewarm water sputtered out of the spout against the tiles and moldy grout. He was in and out in under five minutes.

He yanked on a pair of olive-drab pants and secured his 4-inch blade to the waistband at his side. After pulling on a black, long-sleeved Under Armour shirt, he lifted a large camouflage duffle onto the bed. He took the weapons individually out of the bag, cleaning, oiling, and checking each one. Next, he loaded all his spare magazines with hollow-point rounds. When his firearms were ready, he moved on to his food and personal survival gear.

The Canadian border was only about twenty miles north, but it wasn't an easy trek, so he planned for a two-to-three-day trip, giving himself time to travel carefully. His contact in Canada was supposed to be putting his top-secret information for sale on the dark web, and Ian hoped to be a ridiculously wealthy man by the time he reached Calgary at the end of the week.

He stuffed another smoke between his dry lips while he finished re-packing his survival gear. His muscles ached from too much whiskey. He needed water, coffee, and food, in that order. Fitting a charcoal-gray ball cap over his damp hair, he pulled it down low over his eyes. After he closed the door behind him, he slid an inch-long length of clear fishing-line between the door and the frame just above the deadbolt. If anyone entered his room while he was gone, he'd know it.

Leaving the end unit of the single-story motel, Ian trudged two blocks to a gas station/convenience store where he found a bottle of water, poured himself a large, black coffee, and grabbed a handful of pre-packaged pastries. He waited in line to pay, acting patient though he was feeling anything but. Handing the clerk cash for his breakfast, he gulped down the water before he walked out into the overcast morning back to his room.

As soon as Ian stepped into the cracked and pitted parking lot, he saw him. A local cop was snooping around the parked cars, peering into their windows. Not stopping to ask what the officer was looking for, Ian skirted the lot and walked directly to his room.

"Excuse me, sir. Can I talk to you for a minute?"

Damn! An icy flush of adrenaline flooded Ian's system, and his heart rate spiked. He stopped walking but took time enough to lower his pulse before he faced the cop. "Sure. What's up?"

"Which of these cars belong to you?"

"None. I hitched a ride here."

The cop studied him from behind his mirrored sunglasses. Ian wished he could see the man's eyes, but he watched his body language, anyway. "Where you headed?"

"I'm on my way to the coast of Washington. Hoping to get there before it snows."

Nodding thoughtfully, the lawman's gaze panned over

him. "Got your breakfast, huh? When are you getting back on the road?"

"Once I eat and get packed, I suppose."

"How 'bout I wait for you? I can give you a ride down to Columbia Falls. Save you some time."

The last thing Ian needed was to get stuck with a cop who wanted to take him twenty miles back the way he'd come. "That's a nice offer. Thanks, but I don't want to check out before I have to. You know, get my money's worth by watching a movie on HBO while I have the chance."

"Okay, if you're sure. I'll be here for another fifteen minutes or so, if you change your mind." The cop stood still, most likely waiting to see if he actually had a room at the motel.

"Thanks." Ian unlocked his door and slid inside, hoping to block the cop's view without looking suspicious as he entered his room. He breathed a sigh of relief as he watched the strand of fishing-line flutter to the floor, and he shut the door behind him. Thankfully, he'd left the drapes closed, which hid the gear still lying on the bed.

Ian dumped his pastries onto the small round table by the door and found the TV remote. He scrolled to find HBO and turned up the volume in case the cop was smart enough to check up on his story. He tore open a sugar-glazed pastry and bit into the stale, dry layers, washing it down with a swallow of dark brew. Irritated that he'd have to wait to head north until the cop finished looking for whatever it was he was hoping to find.

A knock startled Ian, and he jumped up from the bed. "Yeah? Who is it?" He crept silently to the window and peeked out. As he suspected, it was the cop. The guy didn't know what was good for him. Why couldn't the officer just leave him alone?

"It's Officer Canaday. Mind opening the door?"

Swearing under his breath, Ian opened the door but held it mostly closed, blocking the cop's view into the room with his body. "What?"

Canaday pressed the toe of his boot against the door, making certain Ian couldn't close it before he wanted him to. "What did you say your name was?"

"I don't think I did."

"Well?"

This guy was pushing his way into the lion's den and didn't even know it. Ian clenched his jaw. He couldn't tell the truth, but lying could be equally dangerous. "John Reddick."

"You got an ID, Mr. Reddick?"

"This feels like harassment. I didn't do anything wrong."

"Didn't say you did. But I'd like to see your ID." Officer Canaday's gaze shifted from Ian's face to the room over his shoulder, and he could tell the second the cop saw the guns. His eyes flared slightly, and his pupils dilated. With that, he sealed his fate.

"My driver's license is in my wallet." Ian reached behind him, but instead of going for his back pocket, he unsheathed his knife. He stepped back, allowing the door to swing open. The unexpected release of pressure caused the officer to lean forward slightly off balance, and Ian took advantage of the movement, yanking him inside the room by the front of his shirt. Simultaneously,

Ian jabbed the blade into the man's gut up to the hilt, then wrenched the tip upward, piercing his heart as he spun him around and kicked the door closed.

The officer's hat and sunglasses fell as his body dropped to the floor. He choked on his own blood. Surprised and confused eyes blinked up at Ian, losing their light before they closed.

"Shoulda minded your own business." Ian wasn't concerned about ruining the dingy carpet, but he did have to get rid of the body. He wiped his blade on the officer's shirt and re-sheathed it. Snagging a second pastry, he stuffed it in his mouth before he peered out of the curtains to see if anyone was around. Seeing no one, he strode to the police car and looked inside. The door was unlocked, and the keys were in the ignition.

Ian quickly scanned the motel windows and the front office again before he opened the door and got in. He turned over the engine and backed up into the spot closest to his door. Popping the trunk, he went back inside his room. He hefted his gear, and on high alert for any movement in the area, he placed it in the backseat of the squad car. All that was left was the body. After wrapping the cop in the cheap bedspread, he hoisted the body over his shoulder and tossed it into the trunk. Canaday, still clinging to life, groaned when he landed. "Don't worry, Officer. You won't last much longer." Ian told him before he slammed the lid closed. He glanced all around to be certain he didn't have an audience. Satisfied, he returned to the room one last time to retrieve the cop's belongings.

Ian pushed his shaggy hair up under the police cap

and put on the mirrored sunglasses. Pleased that he looked like a cop from the neck up and wouldn't cause any suspicion driving the squad car, he carried his last pastry and half-cup of coffee to the driver's side.

He drove out of town along the river until he found a secluded spot to dump the vehicle and after tossing the cop's hat and glasses on the floor, Ian gathered his gear from the back seat, put the car in neutral, and rolled it down the bank. Then he set out on his long hike north through the high country toward his new life.

CHAPTER 8

In the pre-dawn hours, Dirk met with Ranger Lowry at the FBI Field Office to prepare for their search and tracking of Ian McCallum. They received reluctant permission from SAC Reagan to aim their search north of the rest of the team, who were focusing on Yellowstone and Missoula. Dirk double-checked his weapons and safety gear before packing his survival necessities. He had enough MREs to last him an entire week, waterproof matches and a filtered water bottle. One good thing about snow was he'd never run short of water. He could melt as much as he needed and run it through his water filter. The battery and a spare were charged and ready for his satellite phone. He'd purchased an icepick for climbing that he could also use as a weapon if necessary. He packed his tools first and then his cold-weather gear.

His phone buzzed on the desk, and he reached for it. "Hank. What have you found?"

"Since you're making your way north, I contacted

several businesses in a handful of the towns along your route. I shared McCallum's photo and asked if any workers might have seen him in the past two days. I had no luck until I checked in with the Army Surplus Store in Kalispell. On old Vietnam vet works the counter on weekdays, and he thinks he might have seen someone resembling McCallum. He was reluctant to talk to me until I let it slip that the man we are looking for is a traitor. We're waiting for security video from them now, but it will take a while to go through it. Teresa and I will put it on a rush. The chief will help too if she gets to the office in time."

"Where is she? She's usually in by now."

"I think she's over at Tech trying to get answers about the unknown contact on Kendall's Snap account. The good news is there have been no further attempts to contact her."

"Listen, Hank. I need you to keep an eye on my family. Maybe you could stay at my house while I'm gone."

"I'd be happy to, but I'm not sure the boss would agree. She's adamant that she can handle herself."

"I know. I'll talk to her. Anyway, thanks for the info. We'll head up to Kalispell right away and see what we can find out in person. Keep me posted if you see anything on the videos."

"Roger that."

Dirk ended the call and repeated the information to Dan.

"That's as good a place to start as any. If he was in Kalispell, he's headed to Glacier, and that's too close to the border for comfort." Dan hefted his pack. "You ready to go?"

"Let's roll."

Dirk and Dan tossed their packs in the backseat of Dirk's Rubicon and placed their rifles in the far back. Dan's 300 Win Mag was longer and therefore went in first underneath Dirk's more compact M4 Carbine. Both rifles would do the job. A large metal case filled with the various ammo their weapons used sat in the back corner of the Jeep. They returned to the office to fill their thermal coffee mugs and then hit I-90 north toward Kalispell.

A little over two hours later, they rolled into the small town, turning north again on Highway 2. Dirk had a map of the town pulled up on his phone. "Let's start at the Army Surplus." When they located the shop, Dirk noticed the other businesses in the area. There was a Goodwill store directly across the street. If *he* were planning to disappear, he'd use both shops.

They parked near the doors of the Army Surplus store and made their way inside through double glass doors. A rough-looking older man at the counter greeted them. "Let me know if you need any help."

"In fact, we do." Dirk identified himself as a deputy marshal and then showed the man McCallum's photo.

The old guy shrugged. "I might have seen him. It's hard tellin'. Did either of you serve?"

Dan shook his head, but Dirk answered. "Marine Corps—Afghanistan."

The clerk bobbed his grizzled chin. "Army back in

Nam." The two servicemen shook hands. "Then you understand, I wouldn't want to rat out a fellow warrior."

"I get it. Neither would I if the guy were worth the honor. But the man we're looking for is in the business of selling the rest of us, former and active military, out to the highest bidder. He's a bad dude and not worth the loyalty of the brotherhood."

Cloudy blue eyes studied Dirk from behind deep and well-earned crow's feet. "I talked to somebody from the US Marshals this morning, and he said the dude is a traitor. Seems you're corroborating that info, so I suppose I can confirm that the man you're looking for was here yesterday morning. He bought some MREs, a couple of cheap phones and a winter-weight coat. I can't tell you much more than that. He turned left out of the parking lot on foot. That's all I know."

"Thank you." Dirk clapped the man on his shoulder. "And thanks for serving."

"You too, and if that guy really is a traitor, I hope you hurt him when you find him." Dirk nodded, and he and Dan left the store.

Dirk studied the map on his phone. "Highway 2 goes north out of town and will take us through Helena Flats." He glanced up at the overcast sky and flipped the collar of his coat up against a bitter gust of wind. The partners got into the Rubicon, and Dirk turned the engine on so the heater would blow. "I'm gonna check in with my office." He made the call through the car, and it rang through his speakers.

Hank answered, "Dirk, glad you called."

"Is everything okay?"

"Oh, yeah. No news regarding Kendall. The chief requested an unmarked surveillance team to keep an eye out at the kids' schools. But that's not what I wanted to tell you. Teresa found the clip of the video where a man we believe to be McCallum entered the Army Surplus in Kalispell. This guy is good. He wore a hat with a brim and kept his face angled away from the cameras, but we're almost certain it's him."

"Yeah, we just left there after talking to the old vet who rang the guy up. When we showed the clerk McCallum's photo, he positively ID'd the guy."

"Oh." Hank sounded disappointed. "Looks like we're a day late. But we're not a dollar short. Another video came in from the Post Office in Evergreen, which is only a few miles north of the Surplus shop. Guess who showed up there?"

"Good work. That confirms what we suspected; he's traveling north. Why was he at the post office?"

"Looks like he picked up a long, flat box about four inches deep. I'm guessing he picked up a firearm. Though he doesn't open it there."

"Thanks, kid. We'll drive over there and see if we can turn anything up." Dirk ended the call and turned to Dan. "Looks like we're onto him. Now, it's only a matter of time."

"Let's hope we have enough of that before he disappears."

"Right? I'm texting Reagan to let him know we're on McCallum's trail."

A few seconds later, Reagan texted back:

SAC REAGAN

Go ahead and follow ur lead, but one of my FBI teams and their K9 are on a solid trail here in Yellowstone, too. Keep me posted.

CHAPTER 9

Emory didn't tell the kids that she had ordered unmarked details for twenty-four-hour security at home and their schools. There was no need to frighten them any further. And though she was confident that between the security system on Dirk's house and her own skills she could protect them at home, they still had to attend school, and she had to go to work. After confirming the cops were in place, Emory drove to the office.

As usual, she was the first one there. She started a pot of coffee and sat down at her computer. Pulling up all the information she could find on Ian McCallum, she settled in to read every word. Teresa and Hank came in, both said hello and got to work on the digital tracking side of the case. Mid-morning, Emory stretched her cramping back and went to make a cup of Lady Grey tea.

"Hey, Chief," Henry joined her in the break room. "I talked to Dirk a little while ago, and it looks like he and the ranger he's working with are close behind McCallum." He filled her in on the latest details of the pursuit.

"That's fantastic. With any luck, they'll catch him in the next couple of days, and the wedding will go on without a hitch." She took a sip of her tea and closed her eyes hoping to hide the concern in them. If she was honest with him, she'd confess that the wedding was the least of her concerns. She didn't like that Dirk was paired up with a ranger who likely had no experience with a fugitive like McCallum. "While you and Teresa were busy tracking McCallum's movements, I've been scrutinizing his military career during his active-duty status."

"Find anything useful?"

"Not yet... Not really. It seems fairly straightforward. He felt as though the Army had let him down, and so he turned against them." Emory pursed her lips together. "But the thing I keep getting caught up on is the idea that he had to have had help from the inside to escape the way he did. If it were that easy to break away from the FBI, criminals would do it all the time."

"Where's the thought leading you?"

"Backward. I'm looking into McCallum's past to see if I can find any interesting connections, but I've had no luck so far. All I've gained is a sore back and stiff neck."

"Hazards of the trade." Henry chuckled, poured himself a cup of coffee Jond unwrapped a protein bar.

"Boy, isn't that the truth."

Henry's phone buzzed, and he answered it. "Hello?"

Emory watched his expression go from wariness to concern. "Yeah. I'll go over there as soon as I can." He paused to listen. "Of course. Okay, I'll phone you after I see her." He ended the call.

"Is everything alright?"

"I hope so. That was Amy's mother. She just got off the phone with Amy, and during their conversation she had the impression that Amy is off her meds again and might decide to hurt herself."

"You want to check on her."

"Absolutely. Can I get a couple of hours off?"

"Of course, but now that you're divorced, should you be the person checking on Amy?"

Henry's shoulders rounded. "I'm the only one her mom has to call."

"I'm sorry, Henry. This all must be so stressful."

"Thanks. It is, but Amy is Evie's mom, and I'd do anything for Evie."

"I know you would. You're a great dad."

He pressed a flat smile onto his lips. "I'll be back by the end of the day to go over what Teresa and I have found regarding McCallum."

"Good. I'll see you later, then." Emory gave his arm a squeeze and returned to her office.

She reviewed the FBI's collected information on McCallum's post-military years, detailing international missions for which he had been commissioned, along with suspected assassinations and other criminal actions the FBI attributed to him, even though they lacked solid evidence of those. Much of what they reported could have been conjecture or urban legend. McCallum's file read like a Vince Flynn spy novel. Still, she found nothing that helped her understand how he managed to escape FBI custody.

Settling in, she began a thorough search through his college years. McCallum had graduated from West Point, earning a degree in international affairs with a focus on the Middle East. His grades were decent, but nothing remarkable. She scanned through his courses but found nothing unusual. He belonged to the Theta Chi fraternity before accepting a commission as a second lieutenant in the US Army.

Emory downloaded several photos from the file that included some from his graduation, McCallum with his fraternity brothers, his family, and various friends. He looked to be a happy, well-adjusted college student who was more interested in fun than in his education. Basically, a normal, red-blooded American kid.

Next, Emory read through his military jacket. Until the incident that led to his discharge, McCallum had regular, stellar fitness reports—but that was like most officers. Still, he seemed to be an excellent officer, liked well enough by his troops, peers, and commanding officers.

They tapped McCallum for Delta Force when he was a captain, and he was stationed outside of Kabul. That's where everything changed. After that, the records were mostly redacted, but Emory read enough to know that his troop was highly successful until the fated day that six men on his team had gone out on a routine foreign internal defense mission (FID). They were all killed in an IED attack except for one remaining survivor—Captain Ian McCallum—who blamed the Army for the loss and a shoddy follow-up investigation. Shortly after that, he got caught in a CIA sting trying to sell intel. The Army gave him a dishonorable discharge and let him out into the world. From there, most of his work is speculation, but the FBI reports state that he became a mercenary and an assassin for hire.

Lightning flashed and thunder boomed, startling Emory from her research. The sky opened in a downpour. Emory's tea had gone cold, and her stomach rumbled, but she wanted to run a quick check of the men from McCallum's unit who survived their time in Kabul. What had they all been up to these past several years?

While her computer hunted for answers, Emory went to grab the sandwich she'd packed for lunch. She joined Teresa in the conference room to eat. Henry had already left to check on Amy.

"Any chance I can convince you to come help me taste test some wedding cake after work today?" Emory bit into her tuna salad.

"You don't already have that picked out?"

"The design, yes. The flavors... no. Today is the deadline."

"You really like to live on the edge, don't you?"

"Yes, and you do too. Why else did we decide to become Marshals?"

Teresa shook her head and grinned. "I have to pick Tomas up by six."

"No problem. We can leave a little early... say four?"

"Sure. You're the boss."

After lunch, Emory returned to her office and scanned through the printout of the research she'd run.

Her belly roiled when she read that two of the men in McCallum's Delta Force Troop were now in the FBI. It was a normal transition from the military back to civilian life, and she tried not to jump to conclusions, but knowing the loyalty felt by the brotherhood, she couldn't help but make the leap. Was it possible that one, or even both men helped McCallum escape from FBI custody?

CHAPTER 10

Hank pulled to the curb outside Amy's apartment. The complex seemed foreign even though he'd lived there with her once, many months ago. He'd moved twice since then. When he'd first left Amy, he moved in with Dirk temporarily until his partner needed all the extra space in his house for his new family. Hank had happily moved out and subleased Emory's condo from her. The place he lived in now with his infant daughter was far nicer than he could afford, and he figured his boss was cutting him an amazing deal on the rent.

Jumping out of his truck, Hank buttoned his jacket against the cold air. He looked up at the windows of Amy's apartment on the second floor and sighed. He didn't want to face her, but more than that, he did not want her to hurt herself. Hank resolved not to allow her into his emotions and took the outside steps two at a time.

Amy answered his third round of knocking by

opening the door as wide as the security chain allowed. "Hank. What are you doing here?"

"Hey, Amy. Just thought I'd stop by and see how you're doing." Hank cringed at his choice of words. He didn't want her to think he wanted to start anything up again.

Amy stared at him for a moment with eyes that looked bruised with the dark circles under them. She closed the door, undid the chain, and when she opened it to him, she turned away and walked to the living room. She wore baggy sweats and her hair was dirty, sticking out at odd angles. Hank followed her, closing the door behind him.

He remained standing as Amy slumped onto the couch and pulled a blanket over herself. "Are you going to sit down?"

"Uh, sure." Hank perched on the edge of the matching loveseat. "So, how are you feeling?"

She narrowed her eyes and glared at him. "Why do you suddenly care how I'm feeling? Where is Evie? You could have at least brought her here to visit me. You are so cruel."

"I don't mean to be. You know there are restrictions until you demonstrate the ability to stay on your medications." He drew a deep breath. "*Are* you on your meds?"

"Seriously? Are you planning on making spot inspections to see if I'm doped up or not?" Her voice began to rise.

"Amy," Hank held up a hand in a calming gesture. "I care about you. That's not going to change."

"Hmph. Here you are, 'caring about me' in the middle

of the day." She crooked two fingers on each side of her head in air quotes. "You never missed work to 'care about me' before. What's going on?" Her brows crunched together. "Oh, I get it. My mother called you, didn't she?"

"Yes. She's worried about you, Amy. We all are. Everyone wants what's best for you."

"And you all think that drugging me is what's best?" Amy shrieked.

"The medication helps you to regulate your thoughts and emotions, so yes, we believe that what your doctor prescribed for you is best. Bipolar disorder isn't something to mess around with."

"So, you're a psychiatrist now?" she yelled sarcastically.

Hank swallowed his ire and kept his voice calm. "Look, I stopped by because your mom is worried. I can see that you're okay, so I'll leave. But I do hope you'll take your pills. You'll feel better." He stood to go.

Amy rose and grabbed his hand. Tears dripped from her eyes. "Please don't leave. I'm sorry, Hank. I know you hate me, but I'm so lonely. I have no one." Desperation rang in her plea.

Hank's resolve wavered. The hard shell he'd constructed to guard his heart cracked. He put his arms around her. "That's not true. First of all, I could never hate you. And you're not alone either. Your mother loves you, and so does Evie."

She snuggled into his chest. Her hands slid up his back, and she pressed herself against him. "And what about you, Hank? Do you still love me?"

This was not going the way he had planned. "Amy...

we're divorced." He dropped his hands to his sides. "Nothing will change that, but you can count on me if you need me."

Angry again, she pushed him away. "Get out, Hank. I don't need you. I never did, and I never will."

Defeated, he stepped toward the door. "Okay, but will you promise to take your medication? Why don't you do it right now?"

She pointed to the door. "I told you to leave! You no longer have anything to say about how I live my life. Get out!"

"That's true, but you're still Evie's mother. It's important you take care of yourself for her sake, if not your own."

"There you go, being all holier than thou." She turned her back on him and strode down the hall to her bedroom.

Hank let himself out, locking the door behind him. Leaning against the wall, he closed his eyes and let out a pent-up breath. He was no longer married to Amy, but he still felt responsible for her. How would he explain himself to Evie when she got older if he didn't try his best to help her mom?

Speaking of Evie, Hank looked at his watch. If he went back to the office this late, her daycare would close before he could get there to pick her up. He jogged to his truck. Hopefully, the chief wouldn't mind if he got Evie first and brought her to the end-of-the-day meeting with him. He revved his engine. How did other single parents ever manage their schedules?

Hank parked at the front door of Tiny Tots Daycare

and hurried inside. He smiled at the girl behind the entry counter and showed her his ID. She had been watching TV on her computer.

"Hi, Hank." The young woman blushed. "You're early today. Is everything okay?"

"Yeah. I need to pick Evie up before a late meeting at work. It'll be an unofficial 'Take Your Daughter to Work Day'."

She giggled and batted her eyelashes. "You're so funny. You know, if you ever need me to stay after hours with her... or if you need a babysitter outside of daycare times, I'd be happy to help." She leaned forward offering him a view of her cleavage and her hopeful expression sent alarms off in Hank's head. He'd had no idea how attractive single dads with adorable babies were to women. Similar feminine behavior happened to him at the grocery store last week. The thing was, he wasn't currently interested in making room in his life for anyone else. He didn't have enough time as it was.

"Thanks. I'll keep that in mind. But, for now, I just need Evie."

"Oh! Of course. Let me go get her." The woman—Hank didn't even know her name—left to collect his daughter and her things. When she returned with Evie, his daughter's eyes brightened. She smiled and reached for him. His heart swelled. There was no greater feeling in the world. He scooped her up and nuzzled her soft neck, eliciting a baby giggle that changed his whole day for the better.

"Come on, little bug. We're going to Daddy's work." As Hank zipped Evie's coat, he heard a breaking news alert sound from the woman's computer. He peered over the counter and listened. A live video was broadcasting of rescue teams working a scene where a local deputy found a cop's body in the trunk of his car. The vehicle had crashed into a river outside of West Glacier.

West Glacier? Hank ran out the door with Evie and strapped her into her car seat. He had to get back to the office to look into the cop's death and to call Dirk.

CHAPTER 11

Dirk put the call on speaker, and Hank told him and Dan about the murdered cop up in West Glacier. "At this point, we have no way of knowing if this has anything to do with McCallum, but if not, it's a highly peculiar coincidence."

"Yeah," Dirk raised an eyebrow in Dan's direction. "And I don't believe in coincidences. We're just driving into West Glacier now. We'll check things out, and I'll call you later."

"I know that place." Dan pointed through the windshield. "Turn left at the next stop."

Dirk made the turn and from there, and they could see the flashing lights of a sheriff's vehicle pulled to the side of the road about half a mile down. "Looks like we found them. Let's see what we can learn." He parked behind the deputy sheriff's car, and both men stepped out.

Dirk tucked the side of his open jacket behind his holster so that his US Marshal's badge was clearly visible as he and Dan approached the lone deputy. "Saw your lights from the main road. Need any help?"

The deputy looked up hesitantly, scratching his ear as he took in the two men. His eyes rested on Dirk's silver badge for several seconds. "Back-up is on its way."

"Good. Listen, I got a call from my partner in Billings with the news of what you're dealing with here. My name is Dirk Sterling, and this is Ranger Dan Lowry from Glacier Park. We believe it's more than possible the man we're hunting might be your cop killer."

"Oh, yeah? How do you figure? You haven't even seen the body."

"True, but from your initial call to your department, and the fact that this is on the path we think our man is on, it's not a difficult assumption."

"My initial call? How do you know about that?"

"I'm a Marshal. It's my job to know. Also, it was already on the news. You probably have an ambitious reporter with a police scanner. Now, can we give you a hand? Or if you're finished, do you mind if we take a look at the crime scene?"

"I guess. I mean, I'll have to report your being here, and since CSI hasn't arrived yet, I can't let you disturb anything."

"No problem." Dirk and Dan followed the deputy down the embankment to the open trunk of the cruiser. The polyester green, orange, and gold fabric wrapped around the body was pulled away enough to observe the mortal wound in his torso and to see his face. Rigor had not yet set in, which meant the cop's stabbing had to have happened within the last two hours. "Have you investigated the crime scene at the motel?"

"The motel?"

"Yeah, the one the bedspread came from."

The officer cocked his jaw to the side. "No. Not yet, but I'm going to meet the sheriff there as soon as my back-up gets here. How'd you know the blanket came from a motel?"

"First off, hopefully no one would choose that ugly thing for their home, and again... there is a preliminary report on the news and plenty of speculation flying around."

The deputy let out all the air in his lungs, and his shoulders rounded. "You know, Rob Canaday was a good guy. I never thought something like this would happen in our small town."

"No one ever does. I'm sorry. I know what it is to lose a partner." Dirk held the deputy's anguished gaze. "I'm going to glance around in the front seat. I won't touch anything unless it's necessary." He left Dan standing by the deputy and peered into the car.

A paper cup holding a few remaining sips of cold coffee rested in the cupholder. Tossed on the floor, Dirk found a crumpled waxed-paper bag printed with what looked like a shop logo next to a pair of aviator sunglasses and what he assumed was Officer Canady's uniform hat.

He took a photo of the items before he called to the deputy. "Bring some gloves over here." Waiting for the uncertain cop to decide whether or not he should cooperate with him, Dirk encouraged him. "It's a veritable

DNA smorgasbord in here. You're going to have plenty of evidence. I just want to look inside Canaday's cover."

The deputy shook out two blue gloves. "Cover?"

"Yeah. His officer's hat. I took a photo of how everything looks. You should too. Then I want to see if our guy left behind any hair."

"How do you know he wore the hat?"

"Just a guess. Both the glasses and the hat are tossed on the floor. I doubt Officer Canaday would treat his things so carelessly. And both items would hide the identity of the driver if anyone saw him on the road."

"Oh, yeah, I get it." The deputy stepped forward with more enthusiasm.

Dirk snapped on a glove and lifted the hat, turning it over. "There it is." He pointed to a long brown hair sticking to the felt lining. "Canaday has short hair. This strand doesn't belong." Replacing the hat with the hair intact in the exact location he'd found it, Dirk withdrew from the car and pulled off the glove.

"Don't you need to put the hair in an evidence bag?"

"No, I'll leave that to the investigators. I just wanted to confirm that we're on the right trail. We're going to head over to the motel to see what our quarry left behind there. Thanks for giving us access."

The sheriff's car pulled in just as Dirk and Dan drove away. Dan chuckled. "Poor kid. He shouldn't have let us into the crime scene, should he?"

"Not technically, but I'm glad he did. Not only did the stabbing technique confirm that we are on McCallum's trail, the hair sealed the deal. I want to check out the motel room. He might have left a clue to where he's headed."

"Do you think he'd be that unprofessional?"

"He's already showing disdain for the investigators. If McCallum was that careless with his DNA, it means he doesn't think it matters. Sure, it's evidence, but if he disappears, he knows it ultimately won't matter."

"You agree he's moving north, then? To one of the border crossings?"

"North, yes. But not to an official crossing. He'd know they have his photo and information. If I were him, I'd head due north. Straight to the border."

"He'd better have good gear. It's damn cold up that way this time of year, and you never know when a winter storm is going to blow in."

"You know the area, though, right?" Dirk signaled and coasted off the road into the motel parking lot.

"Yeah. As well as any, I suppose."

"Good. I'll rely on your expertise."

They drove past a convenience store not far from the motel with the logo matching the one Dirk noticed on the bag in the cop car. He pulled into the only motel in town and asked the clerk if he had any guests that fit McCallum's description.

"Yeah. That guy is staying in room nine." The man behind the counter returned to his game show on the ancient TV across the lobby.

Dirk knocked on the door. There was no answer. After the second knock, he pushed into the dingy room. A large circle of blood stained the carpet, and someone had stripped the bed of its cover. Dirk moved around the dark spot on the floor and checked the bathroom. Two long hairs in the shower, which looked to match the one he'd seen in the cap, told Dirk everything he needed to know. He didn't need absolute proof at this point, just clues for tracking.

"It's him. Let's get going. We're not too far behind. Call SAC Reagan and give him an update on what we've discovered.

Dan, making the phone call followed him outside and glanced up at the sky. Heavy, grey clouds blocked the sun. "Best if we can catch him before the winter storm comes in."

Dirk thought of Emory and all the plans she and her mom had made for their wedding that was supposed to be on Saturday. He murmured, "With any luck, I'll avoid both winter *and* human storms."

CHAPTER 12

Ian had made decent progress into the depths of Glacier National Park. The sun had shone most of the day, but it was getting late in the afternoon and clouds were rolling in. The wind had picked up, sending an icy chill down the neck of his new extended climate warfighter clothing system—ECWC—coat guaranteed to protect him against temperatures as low as -60 degrees Fahrenheit. He pulled his wool gaiter over his mouth and nose and decided to set up camp before the potential storm came in. He was prepared to weather whatever lay ahead, and a snowstorm added the benefit of covering any tracks he might leave along the way.

He pitched his one-man tent and built a small fire, working to get it hot quickly to minimize smoke. The breeze helped to dissipate that as well. The compact heat was a nice comfort, and he stacked stones into a short wall behind the flame to deflect its warmth to the inside of his shelter.

Ian opened his pack and removed his encrypted,

satellite-powered laptop. He was eager to see what bids had come in so far. The cursor blinked on the blank screen... which remained empty. *What the hell?* He slammed the computer shut and tossed it aside. He'd expected a minimum of ten offers by now. What was the problem? Ian checked his watch. It was only four o'clock in the afternoon. He told himself there was still an hour left in the workday. Two hours if he went by Pacific Time. As if the people he was dealing with cared about work hours.

He heated his dinner as a treat since he'd already put himself up for the night. And he could check the bids again before he slept. He wanted to confirm a buyer before he hiked into Canada, and he expected no fewer than ten bids over twenty-five million. And if he played his cards well, he figured he could get up to thirty mil out of his buyer in China. After he made the deal and the money was safely in his accounts, he would leave the States. He wanted no contact with anyone after he crossed the border. It was the best way to disappear.

CHAPTER 13

Dan directed Dirk to drive past the Ranger's station, up a winding road to his personal quarters, a small cabin nestled in a thicket of pines. "I've got some horses in the barn. We'll make better time if we take them. Do you ride?"

It had been a while, but Dirk had grown up riding horses and rodeoing. Somethings you never forgot how to do. "The last time I tracked fugitives from horseback, I was with two other marshals, and we ran into a bear." He thought back to his partner, Sam, who had been killed trying to protect a judge in Wyoming, and the time before that when Sam, Caitlyn, and he took horses up in the hills to track drug dealing brothers, Raymond and Reggie Burroughs.

"Not uncommon up here." Dan pointed to the tack Dirk would use. In silence, the men got the horses ready for their trek.

The mount assigned to Dirk was a large, sturdy-looking blue roan with a black mane and socks. After they saddled the animals, they led them to the Jeep and loaded their tack down with gear. "You live up here by yourself?"

Dan chuckled. "For now. I can't seem to find a woman who wants to deal with this level of cold."

"Who takes care of your horses when you're gone?"

"Another ranger friend of mine who's posted up here. I'm the only one who lives in the park. Most other rangers live in town, but he swings by on days I'm gone. It doesn't happen that often."

Dirk slid his rifle into a tooled leather scabbard attached to the right side of his saddle. As he packed his last items inside a deep pouch, a Ranger's truck pulled up next to them.

Dan waved as a young ranger stepped out of the vehicle. "Hey, Brian. What's up?"

"District Ranger Milford told me to come get you. We have a missing child in the park. Everyone has been called in. The little girl won't last long at these temperatures if we don't locate her soon."

Dan's brows knitted together, causing a deep crevasse to form between them. His face displayed his internal conflict. He was already on an important mission—one that had to do with national security. But obviously, the thought of a child alone out in the brutal elements tore at him.

"Don't worry about it, Dan." Dirk buckled the leather compartment closed. "Go find the kid. Catch up to me tomorrow. I got this."

"Okay. But let me give you my maps. I marked the paths McCallum is most likely to take. Leave me a trail, and I'll find you as soon as I can. Storm, here, is sure footed and used to these mountains. He'll take good care of you."

"Thanks. We'll be fine." Dirk shook Dan's hand, and the rangers returned to the barn to un-tack Dan's mount.

Dirk located his first path on the laminated map, folded it and tucked it inside his coat. Snowflakes floated through the air, a gentle start to the storm Dirk knew was coming. He pulled his wool cap down over his ears and climbed onto his horse.

He rode by the barn, and Dan stuck his head out of the door. "Hey, I'll try to bring one of the K9 teams with me after we find the child."

"That'd be great. Good luck."

"You, too. And be careful."

Dirk guided his horse into the trees behind the barn. It wasn't long before he came upon a trail which started down by the ranger's station at the entrance to the park and led up into the hills. People had recently traveled on it, which seemed odd. The weather was not ideal for a hike. Dirk dismounted to get a closer look. Large boots left indentations in the snow. These tracks would be easy to follow until the current snowfall picked up and covered them.

It looked to Dirk like more than one person had walked along the trail. He led the grey horse up the path, occasionally crouching to study the various prints. One set seemed older—icier—than the other two, which were still soft around the edges. Could McCallum have made some of them?

Fat snowflakes fell like a dense curtain and Dirk

climbed back in the saddle. He followed the path another mile before it passed by a small meadow where a campfire flickered from a stone ring in the center. Dirk stopped and climbed off his horse. He didn't see or hear anyone, but someone had to be close by. With his training, Dirk didn't think McCallum would be stupid enough to leave an open fire burning for anyone to come across, but he tied the horse and scouted the area anyway. Finding no sign of his target, Dirk took cover behind a boulder and called out, "Hello? Anyone in camp?"

Only the utter stillness of the snowfall answered him, so he moved closer to the fire. Boot prints circled the stones and two separate trails led into the surrounding trees. Nestled behind the tree line against a stone outcropping a black tent had been pitched. Dirk wondered at people who enjoyed winter camping and called out again. "Hello?"

A man's thin face peeked out from the tent flap. "Who are you?"

"Deputy Marshal Sterling."

"What do you want?"

"I'm looking for someone. You haven't seen anyone else hiking around up here, have you?"

The man hesitated. His eyes shifted to something beyond Dirk's right shoulder. A familiar prickly sensation tingled up the back of Dirk's neck. "Uh, no. Can't say I have."

"Okay, thanks. I'll be on my way, then. Stay warm."

As Dirk turned to leave, a searing jolt hit his left arm and knocked him backward a milli-second before he heard the gunshot. In one fluid movement, he unholstered his Glock, dropped to the ground, and rolled into the trees for cover.

The offending rifle fired again, missing Dirk but revealing the shooter's location. Dirk fired, and the cry of his target echoed against the mountains.

"Roley!" The man in the tent yelled. "You hit?"

Roley groaned.

"You shot him!" The thin-faced man bolted from the shelter, zipping his coat as he ran, oblivious that he was making himself a target too.

Dirk pushed himself off the ground and, taking an angle, barreled against the slight man, tackling him. He grunted when he landed face first in the snow. Dirk pressed his knee into the man's lower back and reached for the cuffs he wore clipped to his utility belt. Drawing one wrist and then the other together, he shackled him.

"Who are you?" Dirk rolled the man halfway over so he could see his face.

"I'm not talking to you. You have no right to—"

Dirk shoved the man's face into the snow. He lifted the guy's bound hands away from his back until he stopped fighting. "I asked for your name."

"Sid. Sid Barker. Why'd you cuff me, dude? We gotta check on my friend. You shot him!"

Dirk checked Sid for weapons. Finding none, he undid one wrist, and after having Sid hug a tree, he re-cuffed him in place. "I'll go see about your friend. What'd you call him? Roley?"

With a glare, Sid jerked away. Dirk took a few seconds to assess the wound on his arm. The bullet had barely grazed his skin but sliced a good chunk out of the arm of his coat. He was bleeding, but not enough to stop him from pursuing his shooter.

Holding his Glock in both hands, prepared to fire if necessary, Dirk plodded through the snow toward the origin of the rifle shots. Behind a small berm, he found the gun and a trickling trail of blood leading into a thick stand of aspen trunks. Dusk was setting in fast, but Dirk made out the dark form of a man sitting on the ground, leaning against a thin white tree trunk. His shoulders heaved.

Dirk approached with caution, but the man held no weapons. Instead, moaning, he gripped his left thigh. Roley's eyes flashed up at Dirk. "You got me."

"Wouldn't have if you hadn't shot at me first. Why'd you do that? It's a felony to shoot at a US Marshal, you know."

"I wasn't gonna let you steal our bounty. You should know—the marshals put a bounty on Ian McCallum. We were going to find him fair and square. But I see your trick. You followed us so you could swoop in at the last minute and steal our reward. That's a 100-G you just stole from us."

"You idiot. First off, if you got this close to McCallum, you'd be dead instead of merely wounded. And second, until you broke the law, I was planning to leave you to it. But you had to go and try to kill me. Now, you're going to jail. Do not pass go. Do not collect 200 dollars—let alone a hundred-grand."

Dirk checked Roley for subsequent weapons, and other than a pocket-knife, found none. He tended to the bullet wound. It was a clean in-and-out—painful, but not deadly. Dirk pulled off the man's coat and, using the jackknife, cut a strip of cloth from his shirt to tie around his leg to stop the bleeding. Next, he zipped Roley into his coat with the zipper in the back. He tied the empty arms together behind him. It would hold him until he could get someone to take him to jail.

After walking Roley back to the camp and seating him near the fire, Dirk used his radio to call the Ranger's Station. "This is Deputy Sterling. I've apprehended two men who fired on me. I need someone to come get them."

The voice on the radio responded. "Roger that. What is your location?"

"I'm approximately two miles up from the park entrance on the trail."

"We'll contact the local sheriff and send help as soon as possible, but we're short-handed right now. Any possibility that you can bring them in?"

"No can do. I'm in pursuit of a fugitive. I'll secure the suspects in this location." With all available searching for the missing girl, it could be hours before someone got out there. He marched Sid over and sat him down behind Roley and tied them together, back-to-back close to the heat of fire and he banked the flames.

Angry, Dirk jerked the rope tight. He'd lost precious time and miles because of these two bounty hunters. The marshals set up the reward system to collect information, not to pay unskilled enthusiasts for chasing down dangerous fugitives. There was no doubt in Dirk's mind that he ultimately saved these men's lives.

Dirk dug through his ruck to find an MRE. He offered his captives nothing more than water. While he waited for the police and ate his calorie-rich dinner, he called Emory.

"Hey, how's everything at home? The kids okay?"

"Hi, I didn't expect to hear from you." Her voice warmed him.

"This might be the last opportunity I'll have before I lose coverage."

"The kids are fine. I ordered a detail to watch over them 24-7. It's probably overkill, but I'm not taking any chances."

"Can't hurt. Is Hank staying at the house?"

"He offered, but I can't ask him to do that. He has a baby. Besides, I can handle our home defense."

Dirk clenched his molars together. He knew Emory could take care of herself, but he'd feel better if she didn't have to.

Emory interrupted his thoughts. "I may have found a connection between McCallum and the FBI. I've been thinking he had to have had help to escape from their custody. So, I went digging. Two of the men from his Delta Force unit are currently in the FBI. I don't know if they had anything to do with it, but it's worth looking into."

"Interesting, but be careful, Em. It can be dangerous to start poking around. Why don't you put that on hold until I get home, or at least let the Billings FBI SAC know who you're researching?"

"For heaven's sake, Dirk. You act as though I am unaware of what our job entails. I came up through the ranks too, remember? I'm not a helpless violet." Her indignant argument sparked through the phone and made Dirk smile.

"I know. Sorry. I can't help worrying about you and the kids when I'm so far away. Please stay vigilant."

"Of course, I will. You too."

"Roger that. I've run into a few snags up here, but I'm close. With any luck, I'll be home by Friday." Dirk told her about the missing girl and losing Dan's help, and how he ran into the bounty-hunters. "I've lost some time, but it's dark in the mountains now, and McCallum will have to make camp, too. I'm close to him, Em. Really close. I can feel it."

CHAPTER 14

After dinner, Emory supervised homework hour. While the kids sat around the dining table doing their assignments, she sipped a cup of mint tea to settle her nervous stomach as she thought about her conversation with Dirk. She didn't like that he was on his own tracking McCallum. The elements that far north were dangerous enough. If he was on McCallum's trail, and she believed he was, Dirk could be putting himself at significant risk.

She missed him, and the strength of her feelings surprised her. It made her vulnerable in a way she'd never experienced before. They'd worked together for years, and she hadn't worried about him like this before. But things had changed since they'd become a family... since Dirk had asked her to marry him. She couldn't imagine what she would do if anything ever happened to him.

Shaking off her apprehension, Emory joined Kendall and Jack at the table. Joey had completed his math and spelling assignments and was changing into his pjs. She asked the older two, "Are you both about finished? It's getting late."

Jack pushed his iPad away. "I am. I've had enough history for one night."

"I just need to proofread my essay," Kendall answered without looking up.

By eleven o'clock, the kids were all sleeping soundly, and Emory was putting a few final touches on her wedding vows when she heard a pack of coyotes yapping from somewhere behind the house. She figured they'd caught something for dinner and would settle down eventually. She closed her laptop and stretched her arms up over her head. It was time for bed.

A bang, like a door slamming, sounded from outside. She turned out the lights and peered through the French doors, wondering what was making the noise. A breeze had picked up and had blown something over, though she couldn't imagine what. After a last scan of the back lawn, Emory padded across the carpet to the bedroom she shared with Dirk. She was fairly sure the brewing wind caused the sounds, but with the strange contact Kendall had received, she couldn't relax. She lay on the bed but kept her clothes on and retrieved her handgun from the biometric safe that sat on her nightstand.

Eventually, Emory dozed off, but a loud crash jolted her awake. She gripped her gun with both hands and peered around the corner of the bedroom door. The house was still. She crept to the back door and searched for any movement behind the house. Quietly, she made her way to the window over the sink in the kitchen to look out front. The detail that was supposed to be watching the house was not there. Cold trepidation wrapped its arms around Emory's shoulders, and she shivered. Where were they?

Dirk's home was on the outskirts of Billings on a small acreage that used to belong to a larger farm. Usually, she loved the isolated location, but right now the distance from their neighbors and the missing security detail had her spooked.

The banging sounded again, and she jumped. The noise was definitely coming from the back side of the house. Emory still couldn't see anything, but she wasn't going to wait for trouble to come to her. If someone was out there, she would meet them head on and take care of them as far away from the children as possible. She went to the closet and pulled on one of Dirk's old field jackets and shoved her bare feet into a pair of rubber boots. Unlocking the handgun safe on her side of the bed, she removed her duty Glock and checked the magazine.

Emory peeked in the children's bedrooms to make certain they were safe before she slid out the front door, locking it behind her, and circled wide before she turned toward the back of the house. It was difficult to push open the gate to the backyard. The wind fought fiercely against her progress, but the moon was bright and lit her path. Long ghostly shadows stretched and waved over the ground as she made her way across it keeping inside their cover.

She moved toward the old outbuilding that Dirk used as a workshop. He planned to turn it into a barn someday and maybe get a couple of horses for the kids. He wanted chickens, and a cow, too. Farmer Dirk was a strange concept for her, and she grinned despite her fear.

If someone was hiding out there, he was probably inside the shop. Her heart careened against the walls of her chest as she approached the old, weathered door. She should have called Henry before she came outside. It was reckless to prowl around on her own, but she hadn't wanted to wake him. Besides, what would he do with little Evie if he came to back her up? Emory drew in a slow, stabilizing breath. She released it in a single gush and forced her feet forward. She had been full of bravado when she was on the phone with Dirk, but it had been a long time since she had worked in the field, and her skills were rusty.

Emory approached the splintery door of the building and, inch by inch, she pulled it open just enough to slide herself through. Startled by the up-close noise of the banging she'd heard from the house, she spun toward the sound. Without the benefit of the moon, it was completely dark inside the building.

BANG! A gasp of alarm tore from her throat as she looked up, aiming her weapon with both hands. At the top of the wall, a broken board left a gaping hole and when the wind blew, it lifted a corner of metal siding that hung from the adjacent wall. When the gust let up, it slammed back against the wood.

Groaning at her overreaction, the tension in her shoulders eased, and Emory went in search of a hammer and some nails to secure the noisy panel. She felt her way to the door of a closet in the corner of the building where Dirk kept his tools. When she opened it, something squeaked and ran out over the toe of her boot. Something larger followed it in hot pursuit. Emory screamed and swung her gun toward the movement.

Collapsing against the wall, she laughed at herself. "I almost shot that poor stray cat!" Breathing hard and humming with adrenaline, Emory switched on the light in the closet and found the hammer and nails she needed to quiet the banging metal.

She propped a metal ladder against the wall and climbed up toward the offending metal. Pounding a handful of nails into its edge, she fixed her noise problem. When she finished, she hurried back to the warmth of the house. She checked the children, once again, finding them deep in the sleep of the innocent. She smiled at their blissful forms and released a breath of tension. Returning her gun to the small safe attached to her nightstand, she kicked off her boots and tossed her coat on the floor. She snuggled under the covers but couldn't sleep. Letting her imagination run away with her had caused all the fight-or-flight chemicals to flood her system, and her body refused to let down its guard.

After an hour of flopping from one side to the other, Emory turned on the lamp and pulled her computer from her bag. If she couldn't sleep, she would use the time for work. She opened the files she had created about Ian McCallum's two FBI connections.

The first was a man named Tim Cunningham, who was currently an FBI field agent in Florida. Ian met him at his first duty station in the Army. The second, and more interesting link was Dale Preston. He was an agent in the Colorado Springs field office. Of course, that didn't mean that Preston had access to McCallum while he was incarcerated at the Federal Bureau of Prisons detention facility in Englewood, where he escaped. But it certainly didn't mean he *didn't*, either.

Emory began a broad search into Agent Dale Preston's history. She could only get so much information on her personal laptop, but what she found erased all hope of sleep for the rest of the night.

CHAPTER 15

Ian hadn't slept well. Not only because of the bitter cold, but because of his disappointment and anxiety over the state of his financial situation. His plan was to be a multi-millionaire by now, but as of last night there were no bids for the top-secret US military information. These kinds of secrets had an expiration date. Didn't his buyers understand this?

He crawled out of his sub-zero sleeping bag and rolled it tightly to fit into his pack. His back hurt, and his hands were stiff. He was getting too old for this. Ian let his mind travel to the tropical Shangri-La he'd dreamed of— where his white stucco mansion sat mere yards from a brilliant turquoise surf. He deserved to retire to a secluded paradise where he could recover from his violent life. He was so close.

Filling a tin cup with freshly fallen snow, Ian heated it over a tiny fire until the melted flakes boiled. He added a packet of instant coffee, sipping the bitter mix to warm himself from the inside. Rehydrating his breakfast took a little longer. Powdered eggs and dried ham weren't his favorite. The meal was too salty, but it would give him the energy he needed for the day.

He opened his field laptop to check if any bids had come in overnight. Two had, but their offers were so small they were laughable. China remained silent. A burst of anger roiled up inside him so fast it made him choke on his coffee. In his frustration, he tossed the hot liquid onto the ground. As soon as the fluid left his cup, he realized it was a stupid thing to do. If anyone worth their salt was following him, they would see the melted snow, and the instantly frozen brown droplets of coffee against the pristine white.

After wiping leftover crumbs of egg out of his beard, Ian packed up his camp. He covered up any signs of his fire and dusted over the area with snow from under the trees to hide his tracks as best he could. If he believed in a god, he would have prayed for another fresh covering. Or at least a stiff wind. Either would do more to cover his marks than he could with a pine-needle sweep.

His computer dinged, and Ian rushed to read the encrypted communication. A direct message from his Canadian contact blinked on his screen. He opened the note.

Bid from Chinese imminent, but he wants to meet you in person in Eureka, Montana tomorrow before he extends the offer.

Ian slammed his laptop shut and tossed it in the general direction of his pack. Even if he wanted to, he couldn't get to Eureka in one day. Paranoia pressed in on his thoughts. What if this was a trap? He couldn't afford to get captured. He got to his feet and paced between his gear and the firepit, not thinking about how difficult it would be to cover the snow-packed trail he made.

Meeting the Chinese agent in a place they chose was far too risky. He strode to his stack of supplies and grabbed his computer to compose a response to the Canadian.

Not possible. Will meet the Chinese in Canada once I cross the US border. I'll inform him of the exact location when I get there.

Ian pulled up a map of Canada north of where he would enter the country, searching for a perfect location for the rendezvous. Several minutes later another incoming message dinged.

No go. Operative insists on meeting you tomorrow. Send me a GPS location and he will come to you. Exchange of funds for your info will not happen until after you arrive in Canada. This is his way of vetting you. If you don't agree, the deal is off.

Ian had no choice. If he wanted the big payout—and he had to have it—he'd have to play by their rules. It would slow him down, but at least they were willing to come to him. He would have to scout out a safe place for the meeting, so he responded:

Roger. Will send coordinates tomorrow a.m.

Ian had to find a location for the operative to drop into and a nearby spot where he could watch from a distance to guard against an ambush. The extra day would cost them, too. For the inconvenience, his price just went up.

CHAPTER 16

Normally, Emory would have gone into the office before dawn, but now that she had kids to care for, she had to bide her time. She supervised their getting dressed, breakfast, and the gathering of their school items. Careful to check her watch only a third of the times she wanted to, by 7:30 she wrangled them all out the door to catch the school bus. The accordion doors closed, and the yellow behemoth coughed black exhaust as it chugged away from the curb. Emory waited for the undercover cop car to pull in behind them before she left the house. After they left, she called the police department.

"Seargent, this is Chief US Deputy Marshal Grey. You assigned a detail to cover my house around the clock, but they were nowhere to be seen last night at midnight."

"That's strange. Let me put you on hold for a minute while I check on what happened."

Emory waited, tapping her fingernails on the kitchen

counter. After much longer than a minute the Sargeant returned to the call. "I apologize, ma'am. Apparently, they ran into town for coffee and some food. I have counseled them on showing up to their shift prepared. I can assure you this won't happen again. I trust everything was safe and sound while they were gone?"

She wasn't about to admit to her nocturnal adventure with the loose metal sheeting or the cat and mouse. "Luckily, everything was fine, but gaps in watching my kids cannot happen. Is that clear?"

"Yes, ma'am. I assure you my officers will be with them around the clock."

Teresa and Henry were both at the office when she got there, which she was unaccustomed to, but at least they had already brewed the coffee.

"Sorry I'm late." Emory grinned. "Never mind, this is going to be my new norm, I think. I want to be home with the kids in the morning."

Hank checked his watch. "You're not even late, Boss. At least not according to what most people consider a normal workday."

"Well, the morning meeting is in just a few minutes. Everyone ready?"

"Yes, ma'am." Henry bobbed his head and gathered items from his desk.

Teresa pushed away from her workstation. "I brought donuts in this morning."

"Yes!" Henry pumped his fist. "I didn't have time to eat anything yet. Evie had a diaper explosion right before we left for day-care."

Emory's heart warmed as she watched over her office family. They were missing Dirk—*she* missed him—and he left a big hole, but they had work to do.

When they gathered around the conference table, Emory asked for their reports on Ian McCallum. Henry briefed them on the cop killing in West Glacier. Emory began her report on McCallum's past connections with FBI Agent Tim Cunningham in Florida and Agent Dale Preston in Colorado Springs. She brought up a Delta Force unit photo on the smart screen when Henry's phone buzzed.

He glanced at the screen. "Excuse me, boss. I have to take this." He stood and rushed from the room.

Emory watched him go and swung her gaze to Teresa. "I'll need your help to dig into these connections, especially Preston."

Henry stuck his head in the doorway. "I have to go. That was the hospital. Amy is in the emergency room."

"What happened?" Emory rose to her feet. "Is she okay?"

Henry closed his eyes briefly and swallowed before he spoke. Emory held her breath. "I don't know. It sounds like she might have tried to hurt herself."

"Go. Keep us posted and let us know how we can support you."

"Thanks." Henry's usual boyish face had gone pale and haggard as he dashed out of the office.

"Poor guy." Teresa selected a glazed donut with sprinkles. "He can't get a break. Why is the hospital calling him, though? Shouldn't they have called Amy's mom?"

"She probably never changed her emergency contact number. I hope she's alright." Emory sipped her coffee, thinking about her young deputy. "Henry is under a lot of stress these days."

Teresa wiped crumbs from her mouth. "Have you heard from Dirk?"

"Yes, last night before he hunkered down for the night. He's tracking McCallum into Glacier National Park. The Ranger Service pulled the ranger he was working with off the case temporarily to assist in helping find a missing child, so Dirk's alone."

"Are you worried?"

"Always." Emory sent her a wobbly smile and pressed her palm against her stomach. "Let's get to work digging into the lives of Cunningham and Preston. Who do you want to investigate?"

"I'll take Cunningham." Teresa returned to her desk, taking a chocolate frosted donut with her.

Emory moved to her office and began a deep dive into Agent Preston's past. Year by year she read each of his fit-reports, studied photos, and followed his military career back to the beginning. He spent an admirable stint in active duty that began when he graduated from West Point. Emory read the pages of his graduation yearbook, which contained his class photo. The faces were too small and too similar with their high-and-tight haircuts and solemn expressions for her to recognize anyone. But the individual photos were a different story.

First, she looked up McCallum. He was a handsome, clean-cut young officer. Where had things gone wrong? She scrolled forward to the Ps, searching for Dale

Preston. A wave of deep satisfaction washed over her when she found him. McCallum and Preston were in the same class at West Point. Emory studied his face. Fair hair framed the top of his head, and his blue eyes stared straight into the camera. His image didn't raise any alarms, but neither did McCallum's. She continued to pore through the pages, looking for evidence of a friendship between the men.

In the back pages of the book, she found a collage of photos taken throughout their graduation year. The captions referred to several groups collectively as the West Point Mafia. One group comprised athletes. Another was called the Napoleon Club. Emory researched that one and found it was a historical association whose membership was by invitation only. It seemed to be focused on military genius, which made her wonder.

She recognized the face of one of the graduates in the Napoleon Club photo—Dean Milford. He went through Marshal Training with her. She searched for him in the USMS directory and found that he was working in New Orleans. Emory picked up her phone.

After the initial greeting and teasing, Emory asked Dean if he remembered Ian McCallum.

"That dirtbag? What a disappointment. He was a good soldier as far as I knew, but I heard he's become a traitor now."

"Yeah. He was arrested, but he recently escaped from FBI custody. We're trying to hunt him down now. Do you also remember a guy named Dale Preston?"

Dean hesitated. "In fact, I do. He was friends with

McCallum. Him and another guy, whose name I can't remember right now. They were thick as thieves."

"Did you ever hear of a group at West Point called the Napoleon Club?"

"Oh, sure. That was the club for the super smart dudes." Dean chuckled. "I was obviously not invited."

Emory laughed with him and then said, "You're mentioned in a description of one of the club's photos in your yearbook."

"Huh. I don't remember that. It's probably because I was friends with some of the members."

"Do you know if either McCallum or Preston belonged to the club?"

"I can't say for sure, Em. That organization was draped in secrecy. If I were guessing, I'd say Preston might have been, but I can't say for McCallum."

Emory studied the photo of McCallum and Preston with their arms around each other's shoulders as they ducked into a stone building. "Okay, Dean, thanks. You've been a big help."

"Any time. You be careful poking around in that club roster, though. You never know what you might find."

"What do you mean?"

"Some of those guys are heavy-hitting politicians, and I suspect a few of them might be rubbing shoulders with the deep state."

"Duly noted. Thanks, Dean."

"Okay. Be safe."

"I will. Let's talk again soon." Emory ended the call and sat back against her leather chair, lost in thought. It was a reach, but bonds built in the early years of a career can be the strongest. She considered calling Agent Preston in Colorado, but she'd rather speak to him in person. She wanted to watch his face when she asked him her questions. But she agreed with Dean. It could be dangerous to single him out, so she decided to take Henry with her.

CHAPTER 17

Kendall climbed the bus stairs before her brothers. Joey sat in the front with the other elementary school kids. She and Jack made their way to the back half with the highschoolers. Before she found a seat, she noticed a car parked on their street turned and followed the bus. This wouldn't be unusual if they lived in the suburbs, but out in the country where Dirk's house was, they didn't have any neighbors.

She nudged Jack and pointed at the car with her chin. He tilted his head and looked out the window in the direction she indicated. "What?"

Kendall found an empty seat and sliding into it, she pulled Jack down with her. She leaned close to his ear. "Who is that? As soon as we got on the bus, they did a U-turn and are following us."

"Paranoid, much?" Jack turned sideways on the bench seat to face his friends.

Whispering to the back of his head, Kendall said,

"The word is cautious. Especially after getting that weird Snap."

Jack's back straightened and he peered through the glass, taking a longer look. "They look like cops, Ken. I'll bet you my lunch Emory ordered them to spy on us."

Kendall looked again. Jack was right. The men in the car were clean cut and stiff looking. She relaxed a little. "You're probably right." She searched her pack for her phone and earbuds, until she remembered Emory still had her phone. *Great.* How was she going to get through the day without her phone?

Kit, a girl she'd met in her biology class tugged on Jack's arm. "Switch me spots."

Jack's neck grew ruddy and he gave Kit a goofy grin. Kendall rolled her eyes. "Move!"

Her brother changed seats but took his time passing by the pretty blonde girl.

Kit plopped down beside her. "So, who are those dudes following the bus?"

Kendall's stomach hardened. "What do you mean?" She made a show of looking around.

"You know, the car behind us. Look." Kit pointed to the car behind the bus.

Kendall shrugged. "How should I know?" She dug around in her pack to distract Kit. "Did you do your biology homework?" She wished she didn't have to pretend—wished she could be herself and tell the truth about herself to a best friend. But that was never going to happen. She had to play the role given to her so that she and her brothers would stay safe.

"No. I hate science."

"Yeah, me too." Which wasn't strictly true, but she didn't want to be a dork.

"So…" Kit pressed Kendall's shoulder with hers. "Do you know Ryan Sorenson?"

Kendall's heart jumped and her neck heated. "Um… I don't think so." She pretended not to know the boy, though she'd actually met him last semester in her English class. He'd acted like he didn't care about the class, but he was the only one who could answer the questions about Shakespear's Twelfth Night. His answer was crass, but it was correct. Then he had caught her looking at him and he winked. His attention had made her feel warm all over.

"Sure, you do. He's the first-string quarterback, silly."

"Oh! The cowboy dude?"

"Most guys up here are cowboys, Kendall." Kit rolled her eyes and laughed. "But, yeah. The super cute one."

Kendall laughed with her. "Yeah, I know who he is, but I've never met him."

"Well, that's all about to change! He told my boyfriend, Austin, who's Ryan's best friend, that he likes you! You're so lucky!"

"How can he like me. He doesn't even know me." Kendall thought of Fletcher and her heart pinched. She wondered if he ever thought of her, too. Hoping against hope that the Snap was from him but doubted it. He was told that she'd died along with all her friends in the massacre at her friend Esme's house in Connecticut. The only ones who knew she survived were the Ukrainian mobsters she ran from… was still running from.

"He likes what he sees, I guess." Kit giggled. "He wants to sit with you at lunch today. Will you do it?"

"I don't know. I'd feel weird. Doesn't he sit with the team?"

Grinning, Kit gave her a poke. "I thought you weren't sure who he was."

Kendall couldn't help the smile that took over her face. "I mean... I know *who* he is. But I don't *know* him."

"So? How about a lunch date with the school's sexiest boy?"

"Kit! What about Austin?"

"I'm going out with Austin, but I didn't go blind. Ryan is so hot!" She fanned herself with her fingers and Kendall's face grew warm. "So... can I tell Austin you said you'd sit with Ryan?"

"You can tell Austin that Ryan can sit with me, if he wants."

Kit burst out laughing! "I love it! You go girl!"

The bus pulled up in front of the high school and the driver opened the door. Jack led the pack of kids from the back through the aisle toward the door. He gave Joey a playful shove on his way past. Kendall followed, smoothing her youngest brother's cowlick down.

"See you after school." She smiled at him and hopped down the steps. As she rounded the bus, she looked for the car that had been following them. It was on the street, since it couldn't drive in the circle drive for the busses. Taking a deep breath, she waved at the men. They both looked away. Yep, they were following them alright.

CHAPTER 18

Dirk woke early. He hadn't slept well during the frigid night and had finally drifted off around 4:00 am only to bolt awake at five. It was still dark, so he took his time, allowing himself a hot cup of instant coffee and an MRE to fuel his day. He made a sandwich out of his sausage patty and maple muffin, then squirted the peanut butter packet straight into his mouth before he consumed the bacon and hash browns. The purpose of the meal was caloric energy, and he made sure he had enough.

Even before the sun rose, Dirk worked in the predawn light to pack up his gear. He gave grain to the horse and loaded the saddle with his supplies. He had mercy on the bounty hunters and fed each of them a protein bar and left them wrapped in a space blanket.

"Rangers will be here to get you guys in an hour or two. I'll stoke the fire before I take off."

"You can't leave us here to freeze, man! That's against the law," Sid whined.

"You'll be cold, but you won't freeze. And it's not only illegal—but stupid—to shoot a federal marshal. Be glad you're still alive."

Roley peered up at him from a face drained of color. "What about my leg? I might never be able to walk again."

"Don't be so dramatic. It's a minor soft-tissue injury on the side of your thigh. And it's already stopped bleeding. Stay cuddled up together, and someone will come to get you soon."

Dirk had no obvious trail to follow from there, so he struck out heading north through the terrain on a path that made the most sense to him, leading his horse rather than riding so he could study the ground more closely. A two-inch dusting of snow had fallen overnight, causing yesterday's tracks that much more difficult to follow, but making today's markings all but impossible to hide.

Two hours into his hike, Dirk came across a spot that appeared as though someone had brushed over the area with a pine bough. It's what he would do if he were trying to cover his camp, too, but there was no actual way to simulate freshly fallen snow. Dirk tied his horse to a branch and studied the location carefully. He knelt near a circular divot in the white crystals and swept away the top layer. Small chunks of burned wood lay uncovered, revealing remnants of a modest fire. Nearby, he found light-brown frozen droplets of coffee. This didn't seem to be the work of a professional, and Dirk second-guessed whether he was following the right trail. But a regular camper wouldn't bother to hide his tracks, would he?

Sweep marks left the camp in two directions, both

paths ending at rock fields where boot prints would be difficult to see. Interesting. Dirk admitted to himself a grudging respect for his quarry. Both trails looked about the same, so he took the one his horse could more easily traverse. They skirted the rocks to the west, and Dirk searched for signs of McCallum crossing the field when he got to the far side.

Not immediately detecting anything, he zig-zagged back-and-forth across the open space searching for any sign that indicated someone had come this way. He found nothing, but not wanting to quit too soon, Dirk pressed on into an opening through the thick woods on the distant side of the meadow. The temperature dropped at least fifteen degrees when he stepped out of the sun. The snow was thinner under the tree canopy, and he perceived that other than some deer and a few rabbits, no one had passed through that way.

He'd already hiked more than an hour up the trail, and not finding any human tracks, he turned back to investigate the other option. Dirk led the horse back across the meadow and around the rocky area toward the path to the camp. As he rounded the rock field, he heard voices and stopped to listen.

"This is totally his camp, dude. Look, there was a fire here."

"Yeah, but it could be that marshal's camp, too."

"Why would he have set up a camp again so soon, you idiot? He's trying to catch McCallum too, remember? If we follow him, we'll be there when he finds McCallum. Then we can swoop in first, grab the wanted dude and turn him in for the bounty reward ourselves."

Dirk shook his head and spat into the snow in irritation. Why had the rangers let those goons loose so soon? They'd assaulted a federal officer—which he had reported. Of course, that didn't seem to hold much weight anymore. The bounty hunters probably gave the ranger some sob story, even though the guy's leg wound was minor, and got a sympathy vote. Or, worse, Dirk himself had done a crappy job securing them and they escaped. Either way, they were out wandering around the mountains making his job harder.

He tied his horse out of sight and crept toward the men who would only thwart his efforts to catch McCallum. He watched them search the camp and decided to cut across the woods to the other path he'd discovered, hoping they wouldn't see any tracks other than the ones he made going the wrong way. Then he could search in the opposite direction without them following him. With any luck, he would lose them altogether.

Cutting through the woods was more difficult than he'd anticipated. The horse was too big to maneuver through the trees, and together they made far too much noise. The last thing Dirk wanted was to alert the bounty hunters. He stuffed the gear he absolutely needed into his backpack and left the horse tied to a tree. Either Dan would follow his trail, catch up to him, and find his horse, or Dirk would get the animal on his way back to the ranger station once he had apprehended McCallum.

Without the horse, Dirk could maneuver through the rocky slope on the east side and look for any sign that McCallum had come through that way. He almost stepped on a rock the size of a softball that had been dislodged from its long-time position and then pressed back into place in an attempt to make it look natural. An animal could have stumbled on it and moved it, but it wouldn't have replaced it. He had found McCallum's trail.

The special forces officer had been careful to step only on bare rocks, not leaving footprints in the scant snow surrounding the stones, so Dirk moved slowly. He went back and forth looking for more signs that McCallum had been there and any clues pointing to the direction he had traveled.

Dirk was on the far northeastern side of the rocky field when he saw it. A faint icy edge of boot tread. The rim of the footprint was slightly more crystalized than the soft snow around it as it caught the sunlight more directly. Dirk glanced up at the position of the sun and estimated he couldn't be more than an hour or two behind his target.

He carefully brushed the surrounding virgin snow over the boot print to cover the track on the outside chance the two bounty goons came by this way. He stood and, finding his binoculars, scanned the river valley below him and the jagged mountain that climbed up from its opposite bank. Panning up and down the mostly frozen water, Dirk searched to see if McCallum had crossed the river.

He found what he was looking for on his third pass. Broken ice at the far edge of the water, and a section of boot tread frozen in the mud, glinted in the sun from underneath a smattering of snow. Was it possible McCallum didn't think he was being followed? He was foolish if he didn't, but it seemed like he wasn't taking the possibility seriously. The traitor wasn't as careful as he should have been in covering his tracks. But his lackadaisical efforts made Dirk's mission a whole lot easier.

Until a bullet screamed through the sky.

CHAPTER 19

Hank tried to drive the speed limit on his way to the hospital as he gripped the wheel and eased his foot's pressure on the gas. He and Amy were divorced, but he still had feelings for her. He felt responsible for her, too. How could he not? He married her with the idea that they had a love that would last a lifetime. And it scared him that she would try to harm herself. He knew that phrase meant attempted suicide. But why? Was her life truly that horrible?

Amy suffered from bipolar disorder. She flip-flopped between depression and manic behaviors. He currently had full custody of Evelyn because Amy didn't reliably take her medication, and this situation gave credibility to the judge's decision. Hank supposed that should make him feel justified, but instead he was heartbroken—for Amy, for himself, but most of all for Evie.

He pulled to the curb at the hospital just past the entrance to the emergency room. He flashed his badge at the security guard so his truck wouldn't be ticketed or towed and ran to the reception desk.

"Amy Flannigan? I'm her, er, husband."

"Oh, good. I have some forms I need you to fill out."

"Sure, but can I see her first? Is she okay?"

The nurse glanced over her shoulder to the closed double doors and then turned back to meet his eye. "I'll tell the doctor you're here." She handed Hank a clipboard with several sheets of paper and a pen.

He accepted the forms and sat on the edge of a chair in the waiting room. His hand trembled as he rushed to answer the questions the best he could. When the doctor emerged from the swinging doors, the receptionist pointed him toward Hank. He stood, bracing himself for whatever the grim-faced, white-haired man was going to tell him.

"Henry Flannigan?"

"Yes, that's me. Is Amy alright?"

"Let's sit down."

Hank's stomach balled into a fist. He set the paperwork on the reception desk and followed the doctor to two chairs apart from the main grouping. Heat rose from his chest and filled his face, and he swayed slightly as he sat.

The doctor leaned forward, bracing his forearms on his knees, and held his hands together between them. "Mr. Flannigan, your wife cut her wrists this morning. The paramedics were able to stop the bleeding, but she has lost a lot of blood. We are giving her blood transfusions and IV fluids to replace the volume, and she's on medications to help stabilize her blood pressure. She is under continuous supervision to prevent her from trying to harm herself again."

"How… Who found her?"

"Apparently, she called her mother to say goodbye. Her mother is here with her now. She gave the nurse your phone number."

"Can I see her?"

"Not just yet. The psychiatrist on call will speak with her first, and then, if he determines it's in your wife's best interest, you will be allowed to see her then."

Hank realized what the doctor was not saying—that Amy's attempted suicide might be because of him or something he did. And he felt the guilt settle heavy on his shoulders. "Okay, I'll wait here. I have to go park my truck, but then I'll be back."

"Good. I'll tell Amy and her mother you are here. I'm sure they'll want to see you soon."

"Thanks, doctor, for… well, for helping her."

The older man offered him a sympathetic smile and nodded before he returned to the emergency room. Hank left to park his truck in the lot and bought a cup of vending machine coffee before he settled himself in the waiting room. He swiped through his texts and phone calls before he dialed the office.

"Billings Marshals Office, this is Deputy Mendez. How can I help you?"

"Hey T. It's Hank."

"How's Amy?"

"Stable, I guess. They won't let me see her until she sees a shrink."

"Sounds like she's right where she needs to be."

"Yeah. I don't know how long I'll be away from the office."

"Of course. Don't worry about it. I'll let the boss know."

"Thanks. Keep me updated with any news about Dirk, will you?"

"You bet."

"Thanks, T. I'll keep you posted too." He ended the call. Cradling his phone between his hands, Hank hung his head. Was there a way he could have prevented this? Amy was sick before they got divorced, but maybe the separation made it worse? Certainly not having Evelyn with her made her sad, but he couldn't allow his daughter to be in danger. It seemed like he was the bad guy, no matter what he did.

Two hours later, the receptionist approached him. "Mr. Flannigan? If you'll follow me, you can see your wife now."

Hank blinked up at her and rose to his feet. He pressed his hand against the tightness in his belly. "Thanks."

He followed the woman through a maze of hallways, and he absently wondered if he'd be able to find his way back out. She led him to a heavy door that required her to swipe her ID so they could enter. They passed a community room on his left where several patients wearing pajamas and robes sat reading or playing cards. On his right was a nurse's station closed in behind a glass window where the receptionist handed him off to a ward nurse. He walked with her down a hallway of closed doors, and when she came to Amy's room, she unlocked it before they could enter.

"Is this the psych ward?"

The nurse inclined her head. "Your wife is here for short-term crisis care." She pushed the door open and entered before Hank. "Hi Miss Amy. Your husband is here to see you. Is that alright?"

Amy's mom stood from her chair next to Amy's bed. "I'll step out." She avoided Hank's gaze as she walked past him and left the room.

Amy looked small and vulnerable lying in the hospital bed. Tears fell down her cheeks when she saw him, but she nodded her consent to Hank's presence, so the nurse left, the lock clicking into place behind her.

"Hey, how are you feeling?" It was a stupid question, but Hank couldn't think of anything else to say.

"I'm so sorry," Amy cried. "I'm embarrassed. I don't know what came over me." She looked him full in the face then, and her eyes appeared hollow and bruised. "Where's Evie?"

"She's at daycare. I came from work."

"Oh, God!" she wailed. "Now everyone knows."

"Amy, no one knows anything. They're just concerned about you."

"And you? Are you concerned?"

"Of course, I am. I don't understand, but I do care about you. I—" He almost told her he loved her, but that would only confuse the issues. He didn't know what to do, so he jammed his hands into his pockets.

"Can you bring Evie to see me?"

"I don't know. I can ask the doctor, but I doubt they'll let kids in this ward."

Her eyes flashed at him. "In the looney-bin, you mean?"

Hank sighed. Even now, the old patterns arose. "No, Amy," he said with all the patience he could muster. "I do not mean that. I'll see what the doctor says, and I'll do what is best for Evelyn and you." If he was honest, he didn't want his innocent daughter anywhere near Amy right now, or anywhere near this section of the hospital, period. He didn't trust his ex-wife not to do or say something damaging. But he would listen to what the doctors recommended.

"Why are you even here? You're not my husband anymore. You have no say over what I do or don't do. And you have to let me see Evie."

Suddenly, Hank wanted to be anywhere but there. "You're right. I'll leave since my being here clearly upsets you." He knocked on the door to be let out.

"Hank! No, I'm sorry. Don't go!" Amy cried from the bed.

The door opened, and without looking back, Hank said, "I hope you get the help you need. Please take care of yourself." Then he left.

Amy's mom walked up the hallway carrying two steaming cups. "Are you leaving already? I brought you some coffee."

Hank took the offered cup. "Thanks. I don't think it's helpful for me to be here. I'm just making things worse. Will you please call me with any updates?"

"Oh, Hank. I'm sorry about all this. I know you're

trying."

"I'm sorry too, Jan. None of this is what I wanted. I—"

She rested her hand on his arm. "None of this is your fault. Amy is sick, and we're going to get her help. I'll call you tonight."

"Thanks."

Hank waited to be let out of the locked ward, and he followed the exit signs to find his way back to the waiting room. He tossed the coffee as he left the hospital; his stomach couldn't handle the extra acid right then. He checked the time on his phone, and the lateness of the day startled him. He'd have to pick Evie up from daycare before he returned to work or he would be late to get her. Hopefully, the chief wouldn't mind him bringing his daughter in again for the last half-hour of the day.

When he got to the office, Hank left the car seat in his truck and carried Evelyn in his arms. Feminine squeals sounded throughout the office as both Teresa and the boss ran to scoop Evie out of his arms. A proud-dad grin spread across his face. "Guess you two don't mind if Evie is here for a little while." He chuckled.

"Mind? We'd rather have her than you!" Teresa elbowed him in the ribs.

His boss's searching green eyes met his. "How is Amy doing?"

"She's safe. Her doctor admitted her into the psych ward to prevent her from trying to hurt herself again."

"I'm really sorry, Henry. You'll let us know if there is anything you need?"

"I don't need anything, but thanks. It wasn't helpful to

Amy for me to be there. Her mom promised to keep me informed."

"So, you won't need to take any time off?"

"No, I don't think so."

"Good. I need you to come with me tomorrow. I want to go speak with FBI Agent Preston. He's stationed at a field office in Colorado Springs. I spoke to his admin and learned he has a meeting tomorrow, so I scheduled coffee with him afterward. We'll fly down in the morning."

"Are you feeling like you need backup?"

"Yes, actually. I'll explain everything on the way."

"Will we be back before six? I have to pick up Evelyn."

Teresa, who was blowing raspberries against his daughter's neck, eliciting delicious baby giggles, paused her game. "I can pick Evie up if you're not back in time. Tomas would love it!"

Hank's shoulders relaxed for the first time all day. It was good to be back at work—with his real family. "That'd really help, T. Thanks. I'll call the daycare to let them know you're coming and to get you on the pick-up list. I can try and have my mom come to stay again, too. I'd like to join Sterling in the field. What are you doing about your kids, Chief?"

"Kendall knows I'll be home late and besides, the police detail will be there watching over the house." Emory's smile was unconvincing and Hank wished, not for the first time, that he could be in two places at once. If anything happened to Dirk's family while he was gone, Hank would never forgive himself.

CHAPTER 20

The next morning, Ian struck out to find a spot for the Chinese operative to drop in. Who knew why the untrusting East Asians demanded they meet in the field. Why couldn't they wait until he was safely in Canada? The operative was probably planning to steal his computer and leave him dead in a snowdrift. He hiked on while considering his options.

Finally, he came upon a clearing that was barely large enough for a helicopter to land in. He sent his contact the GPS coordinates. As soon as he ended the com, Ian bolted for the trees. He shrugged off his pack, removed his cell phone, and stashed his bag in a group of rocks nestled together at the foot of a giant pine. Remaining hidden in the forest, he sprinted through the forest around the open space to the opposite side and waited there. His potential buyer couldn't take the information if he didn't know where it was, and he'd have to keep Ian alive to get it.

Thirty minutes later, he spotted a sleek black helicopter buzzing through the sky toward the meadow. It hovered for several seconds before it landed. Ian's gut squirmed, as if he had swallowed a dozen eels. The sound of the rotor blades reverberated against the rock-faced mountains, and exhaust polluted the pristine air.

He noted there were two men inside the small craft, the pilot and the man who came to meet him. Ian waited for the operative to disembark. Both men were sitting ducks for each other, but the Chinese man had back up. Taking a deep breath, Ian raised his hands and stepped out from behind the cover of the trees. The slight man, dressed in black leather from head to toe and armed with a QBZ-191—the latest in Chinese military rifles—on a sling-strap over his chest, strode in his direction. The men met at a halfway point, approximately 50 yards from the helicopter.

"Mr. McCallum, I presume."

Ian watched closely for any sudden movement toward his weapon and kept the operative between himself and the chopper in case the pilot became a problem. "That's me."

The Chinese man rested his gloved hands on his hips and, looking around, took in the vast wilderness. "This is certainly an unforgiving part of the world. We would be happy to fly you out of here. In fact, we could negotiate our deal while we are in the air."

No way was Ian getting on that bird. If the guy didn't kill him, he'd end up festering in a Chinese prison somewhere—which was arguably worse than Leavenworth—and they would strip his computer, find all his secret information, and own it for free. "I don't think so. I'm doing just fine out here."

"Suit yourself," the man sighed. "I need evidence that you have the information you claim you do. Once I confirm, I will receive the authorization to make a deal."

"I've already sent proof to your puppet master, and I'm not about to show you the documents out here. I'm sorry to say, but your trip was unnecessary. We could have done all of this over our computers."

"My handler prefers we do business in person. What are you prepared to offer me if you won't allow me to see the full spectrum?"

"Your boss already has all the proof he needs. I'm not going to give you any more reassurances. I didn't invite you out here, remember? You insisted."

The man closed his eyes, steepled his fingers together, touching his lips. He breathed in through his nose as though gathering patience. "I came because we need more evidence of what you're selling than you've previously shared."

"And this couldn't wait until I got to Canada?"

"As I said, we could be in Canada in an hour if you'd accept a ride. Why would you choose to hike through this frozen wilderness when you could fly? You might break a leg and die out here, and no one would ever know.

Ian spat on the ground. "There is no way I'm getting into that aircraft with you." He pointed to the front pocket of his pants. "I'm going to reach into my pocket for my phone. But after showing you what I have there, my price goes up for this inconvenience."

The muscles along the operative's jaw rippled, and his

expression flattened. "You may price yourself right out of a deal."

"I doubt it." Ian showed the Chinese man photos of two documents that he had electronically redacted of any pertinent information. The surrounding text was enticing enough. "As you can see, I have what you want and more. My new price is 50 million."

To his credit, the man didn't flinch. He gazed directly into Ian's eyes until his black orbs made a slight shift. Faster than a cobra, the operative shoved him aside, leveled his rifle, took aim and fired. He turned back to Ian as though nothing had happened. "You have something we want, but not acquiring it changes nothing for us. Our position on the world stage will remain the same as it is now. You, on the other hand, have your life. Losing that would change everything for you. If I were you, I would not press my luck. Our agreement was for 30 million. Consider that generous."

Ian's pulse raced from the unexpected shot. He couldn't concentrate. "What did you just shoot at?"

"Something moved. It won't move anymore. Now, do you agree to cooperate with our original arrangement?"

Ian knew better than to tempt his fate any further. Honestly, he was thrilled with 30 million. "It's a deal." He shook the Chinese man's hand.

"Very well. We will see you in Canada in two days, then. *Zàijiàn.*"

The small man climbed aboard the helicopter, and it ascended, blowing snow and ice crystals in Ian's face.

CHAPTER 21

The bright morning sun reflected off the adjacent building, causing Hank to blink away as he pushed open the office door. "Morning, T."

Startled, Teresa spun around in her chair. "You're here early. Are you feeling alright? Or maybe Dirk's bad influence doesn't affect you when he's not here?"

"Ha ha. Get used to it. I drop Evie off at daycare at 7:00 am nowadays."

"How is all of that going?"

Hank shrugged off his coat and crossed the floor, following the alluring aroma of coffee to the break room for a much-needed cup. "So far, so good. I'm getting the hang of it, I guess. The routine isn't bad when work is eight to five, but as you know, that isn't the norm. I wouldn't have made it this far without Laurie and my mom's help, though. Yours, too. Thanks again for picking Ev up after work today. With any luck, the chief and I won't be too late." Hank filled his mug and took a fortifying mouthful of the stout brew before he carried the pot to Teresa's desk to heat hers.

"Thank you." Teresa took an appreciative sip and smiled. "Being a single parent isn't easy, but you'll get into a rhythm."

"I feel like I should be able to do this on my own. Plenty of parents do it, but all the scheduling and being sure I have enough time with Evelyn before she goes to bed is hard."

"The 'plenty of parents' you're referring to aren't deputy marshals. Your schedule is generally up in the air. I'm always happy to be a third option for you, too. Believe me, I get it. It's why I opted to cover the admin side of the office instead of being in the field. Tomas has only me. If something happened, he'd be alone."

Hank knew Teresa was concerned about the safety aspect of their job. At least Hank's daughter had two sets of grandparents. "Tomas would have me, Dirk, and Emory—you know—if anything ever happened." He gave Teresa's shoulder a reassuring squeeze and shook off the uncomfortable thought. After returning the coffeepot to its stand, he sat down to work. "Anything new come up on McCallum?"

"Nope. I've been trying to build a pattern of life for him through Fog Reveal," Teresa said, referring to their controversial, but powerful cell phone tracking software, "but the guy is a true professional. I can find him, but he has no repeatable actions to latch onto."

"Any word from Dirk?"

"No. If he calls, he calls the boss."

Hank opened a new search through the USMS

Missions System. "I'm going to dig a bit deeper into his military background."

The office grew quiet except for the keyboard clicking as Hank and Teresa focused on gathering all the information they could on Ian McCallum. Through facial recognition bringing up images that people had posted anywhere online, Hank kept busy with thousands of pictures. Most were not helpful, but there were a hundred or so that he set aside to enhance and study more closely. Most of those were official military photographs of McCallum at military events. There were hardly any personal shots that spoke to the man's career as an operative. Hank agreed with Teresa's assessment. The guy was good.

Two pictures caught Hank's eye. He enhanced them both and studied them side-by-side. In one, the photographer caught McCallum in the background of an Army unit picture. He wore desert ACUs and was in what looked like an intense discussion with an Army colonel. They weren't the focus of the photo, and Hank almost missed it. He ran a facial ID on the colonel. While he waited for that information to come through, he stared at the second image.

This one was at a formal military dinner, possibly a dining-in. The men were all in their dress blues. The picture was from someone's phone camera, and they had posted it on Facebook. McCallum was not the subject of this photo either. It was of four apparently inebriated officers with their arms around each other's shoulders, holding mugs of beer and laughing at the person behind the lens. Again, in the distant background, Hank found

McCallum, his head bent together with the same colonel.

Hank's computer dinged with the senior officer's identification. Steve Webber, Army Colonel Retired. A third man was part of the conversation, but his back was to the camera. Hank ran a search on Colonel Steve Webber and found that he was currently a weapon systems consultant to the Pentagon. His blood ran cold. "I think I found something, T."

"Yeah? What?"

"A likely connection between top-secret weapon systems and McCallum. I might have stumbled upon the source of the information McCallum is trying to sell." He second-guessed himself. "I mean, it could be nothing, too."

Teresa stood and looked over Hank's shoulder at the photos on his monitor. "Better call the boss."

"Where is she, by the way? The chief's usually the first one in the office."

"She decided to drive the kids to school today. She'll probably be here any minute, but this shouldn't wait."

"Roger that." Hank reached for his phone and dialed Emory.

"Hey Hank, what's up?" Chief Grey answered.

"I think I found the link between McCallum and his—"

Tires squealed, and his boss shouted expletives at someone right before the call disconnected.

CHAPTER 22

Kendall hugged Emory when she dropped her and Jack off at the high school. "Thanks for driving us today. I'm just nervous, but I'll feel much better when you find out where that weird Snap came from. And thanks for letting me have my phone back."

"You're welcome. But be safe with it. I'll feel better when we hear back from Tech, too. Have a great day, you two. Remember, I won't be home until later tonight. If you need anything, call Teresa at the office. And you have her personal cell number too, right?"

"Yeah. Plus, those undercover cops are watching the house, too. We'll be fine."

Emory did a double take. "You guys know about that? I was trying to protect you without making you afraid."

Kendall grinned. "I know. But they're pretty obvious."

"Smart kids!" Laughing, Emory waved. "I'll try not to be too late." The kids both shut their car doors and waved back at her before they walked up the sidewalk and entered the building. "Next stop, your school." She smiled at Joey in her rearview mirror.

Teresa's son Tomas was at the front doors of Joey's elementary waiting for him. The boys had become friends months ago, and now they were hardly ever apart. Emory barely got a "bye" from him before the boy jumped from the car, slammed his door, and raced toward his friend. Emory chuckled, happy to see how well the little guy was adapting to his new life with her and Dirk. It had been easier for him than for his older siblings, understandably.

Listening to Yo Yo Ma play a Chopin nocturn on his cello, Emory made her way onto the highway, hoping to cut her commute time more than if she stayed on the city streets. A call came through her dashboard from Hank, interrupting the music. "Hey Hank, what's up?"

"I think I found a link between McCallum and his—" the car in the next lane sideswiped her. She gripped the steering wheel and forced her sedan back into her lane. Fear-fueled fury engulfed her. "What the hell? What are you doing! Watch out!" The old model black Bronco that hit her had an orange and red stripe across the doors, and its tinted windows were so dark Emory couldn't see the driver.

The hulking vehicle turned into her again, and Emory had to fight to keep her car on the road. Her phone flew from its holder, crashing to the floor. A stream of words she wasn't proud of spewed from her mouth. She sped forward and glimpsed the driver through his windshield. He was a swarthy man with rough features, wearing a dark beanie and a heavy black coat. That was all she had time to observe before he hit her again and her car veered off the shoulder onto the grass. She braked and corrected the direction of her vehicle, steering back to the pavement. The Bronco surged forward but then slowed to match her speed. The man cranked his wheel and rammed her another time. Emory held on tightly, slammed on the brakes, and maneuvered behind the Bronco, passing it on the right side, and then floored the engine. She surprised him by exiting the highway and bought herself a few precious seconds to call 911 with the buttons on her steering wheel.

"Billings Police Department. What is your emergency?"

"This is Chief US Deputy Marshal Grey. I am in my vehicle traveling north on I-90 toward Billings. A man in a black Bronco is trying to run me off the road. I need assistance right away!"

Soon the Bronco reappeared in her mirror. She accelerated ahead of him, praying they wouldn't hurt any innocent drivers in the chase. Her heart raced as she sped up the on-ramp on the other side of the intersection. Fortunately, a local cop was manning a speed trap from a hidden position there, and he fired up his lights and siren. Once the squad car joined the race, the Bronco peeled off, abruptly exiting the highway with the cop on its tail. Emory called emergency dispatch back and explained what had happened and told them where they could reach her for a statement. Shaken, she drove the rest of the way to the office.

Who could be trying to kill her? Well, maybe not *kill*...

but harm, or at least frighten her, for sure. Her first thought was that it was someone from the Ukrainian mob who had attacked Kendall and her family. Was the mysterious Snapchat message from them? But if so, why would they go after Emory? She shook her head in confusion as the first snowflakes of the season floated through the steel-gray sky and landed softly on her windshield.

She parked in her designated spot and bent to collect all the items that had spilled from her purse when she got hit. Getting out of her car, she viewed the damage on the passenger's side. Grumbling under her breath, she complained, "That won't be cheap, and I'll be surprised if that jerk has insurance." She purposefully chose to be angry over her damaged vehicle than to give into the fear nipping at her thoughts.

Hank jumped from his seat when she entered the office. "Are you okay?"

Emory had forgotten that she'd been talking to Hank when she got hit. "*I'm* okay, but I can't say the same for my car."

"What happened? I heard you cussing someone out and then the phone went dead." Hank helped her out of her coat while Teresa made her some tea. They fussed around her as if she were a child.

Emory told them the story and her concern that the Ukrainians had found them again. "I'll call BPD later to find out if the cop caught the driver. But we need to get going." She checked her watch. "Our flight leaves in three hours."

While she drank her tea, Hank showed her the photos he'd discovered and the obvious connection between McCallum and Webber. "He's a weapon systems consultant to the Pentagon. This could be the leak—the source of McCallum's secret military information."

"Good work, Hank. It could be, but it might also be that they were simply friends or even talking about a mission or something. Keep digging into it, but I'll call my dad's acquaintance, Warren Pole, and see what he knows about Webber."

Teresa sat on the edge of her desk. "Your dad knows the Deputy Director of the FBI?"

"He knows everybody, and I have no shame in dropping his name." Emory grinned. Her phone buzzed, and she rummaged in her messy purse, which she hadn't reorganized yet. "Hello? This is Chief Deputy Grey."

"Hello, Chief Grey. This is Sergeant Marino with the Billings Police Department. I wanted to let you know that our officer apprehended the man who hit you this morning on the highway."

"Fantastic. Who is he?"

"His name is Bill Blankenship. He's a local dirtbag. We're still interviewing him, but it looks like he was a hired stooge. Says he got a cash payment to put some fear into you. He claims he doesn't know who hired him."

"Thank you for keeping me informed. Is there any way you can add a second undercover detail to the one you already have watching my house? I have to fly to Colorado today, and my kids will be home on their own for several hours after school. I'm almost certain the scare tactic was a message regarding them."

"Let me clear that with my captain, ma'am, and I'll let you know."

Emory tossed her phone back into her bag. "Teresa, I told Kendall to call you if she needs anything, but maybe you wouldn't mind just checking in with them?"

"No problem, Chief." Teresa dug the toe of her shoe into the tile floor. "I don't mean to bring up a sore topic, but it's looking like you'll have to postpone your wedding. We've heard nothing from Dirk since Hank called him days ago."

Emory's shoulders drooped under her disappointment. She'd been doing her best to stay positive about the ceremony and not worry about Dirk. "Yeah. I know. I'll call my parents and tell them not to come. But for now, Hank, we need to get to the airport."

They flew into Colorado Springs Municipal Airport and after picking up their rental car, drove directly to the local FBI Field Office. Emory led the way into the small office, nodded crisply to the woman at the front desk and marched past her toward the closed door in the back.

The woman leapt to her feet. "Excuse me, ma'am. Do you have an appointment?" Emory ignored her. "Ma'am, you must have an appointment!"

Emory opened Agent Dale Preston's office door and approached his desk with Hank by her side. "I'm Chief Deputy Marshal Grey from the Montana Region and this is Deputy Flannigan. We'd like to talk to you about your relationship to Ian McCallum."

The face of the man sitting in the office lost all its color. His jaw fell open, and he rose slowly to his feet, gripping the edge of his desk for stability as he swayed. "What relationship? Of course, I know the name. Ian McCallum escaped from federal custody, but I don't know the man personally. And I don't like your implication."

Emory slid her leather tote from her shoulder, setting it next to a chair facing Preston's desk. "May we sit down?" She nodded at Hank; they didn't wait for permission. Emory reached into her bag and pulled out a photo, which she laid on Preston's blotter facing him. "Do you recognize the men in this picture?"

"Where did you get this?" A red blush crept up from Preston's collar, and he loosened his tie for relief.

"The original is in your West Point graduating class yearbook. It looks like you not only know McCallum, but that you were good buddies. Perhaps the kind who stay in touch over the years."

"Screw you."

Hank balled his fists and started to stand, but Emory rested her hand on his arm to settle him. "You'll never be so lucky. But all that aside, you're getting rather worked up, which I find interesting. We only came here to ask you if McCallum might turn to you in desperation or if there is anyone else you remember him being friends with who he might reach out to for help."

Preston rubbed his upper lip and took slower breaths. "I'm not worked up, but I don't appreciate the implication that I'm friends with that guy. I hardly knew him."

Emory slid four more photos she'd copied that showed the men together. "So strange... I've never been in five pictures with someone I *hardly knew.*"

Preston's anger boiled in his eyes as he glared at her. She'd lit the fuse; now it was time to see what would blow. "Here's my card. You'll call me if any names come to mind, won't you? We must find McCallum before he commits treason and brings down anyone who ever worked with him." Emory stood, and Hank followed her out of the office. Before the door closed, she peered through the crack. Preston was already dialing his phone.

CHAPTER 23

Kendall gathered up her notebook and iPad when the bell rang. Her teacher called out a reminder for the homework assignment over the noise of chairs pushing away from tables. She left the classroom in the middle of a rush of kids and made her way through the throng to her locker. Her eyes scanned the taller boys, hoping to catch a glimpse of Ryan.

The day she'd agreed to have lunch with him, she had sat at a table with Kit and three other girls from the cheer squad. Ryan picked up his tray from the cafeteria and strode across the room to her table. He waited until one by one, the other girls all left giggling at his confident approach.

"Hi. I'm Ryan. Mind if I sit down?"

Kendall's face had heated furiously, and she died inside knowing it was bright red. "Sure."

He had swung his long legs over the bench and sat right next to her, leaving the rest of the table open. No one tried to sit with them. "And you're Kendall, right? You were new last semester."

"Yeah."

"Jack Miller's sister?"

"You know Jack?"

"Sure. He's the kid trying to win my spot on the team. It won't happen, but when I graduate, he'll be the starting QB. No doubt. He's good."

"Thanks." Kendall had no idea what to say to Ryan, but he didn't seem to mind.

"Where did you move here from?"

Ugh. She hated having to remember the lies she was forced to tell everyone. "Ohio."

"Do you like it here?"

"So far. It's pretty, I guess."

"We should go on a hike in the mountains. It's beautiful up there."

Was he asking her out or just talking about what he loves about Montana? "I... I mean, that would be cool."

"Really? Awesome. What are you doing on Sunday afternoon? I could go Saturday, but it would have to be later cuz I have to work."

"I'll have to ask, but I'd like to go." She smiled at him. He was easy to talk to and her shoulders unknotted themselves. "Where do you work?"

"On a ranch."

"Really? Are you a real cowboy? What do you do there?"

Ryan laughed. "A *real* cowboy? What's that supposed to mean?"

"Just that lots of guys wear cowboy boots, but that doesn't mean they've ever been around horses or cows."

"True enough, but not for me. I was practically born on a horse." He gazed at her and her tummy flip-flopped. "Do you ride?"

"Me?" Her eyes widened. "No. I mean I took a couple of lessons when I was kid, but that was English."

"That's still riding, though you won't find any English saddles where I work. Maybe we should go on a trail ride, instead?"

"I don't know. I probably don't remember anything from those lessons."

"I could teach you."

"I'll ask if I can. You might have to meet my..." she hesitated. Should she say foster parents? Or would that bring on another slew of questions she didn't know how to answer. She'd never called Emory and Dirk her parents before. It felt too weird. "I'll have to get permission."

"Sure. You can text me." His face brightened with a warm smile. "Can I have your number?"

That was how her new obsession with Ryan Sorenson began. He took up a ton of space in her mind and hours of her time as she stalked him online. Kendall stopped at her locker and spun the combination dial. A shadow cast over the numbers and she looked up to see Ryan leaning against the locker next to hers.

"Hey."

"Hi." She inhaled. He smelled so good she swayed toward him. He cupped her shoulder and ran his hand down her arm until his fingers twined with hers.

"Hey, you two." Kit approached them. "Are you guys going to Stetson's party this Friday?"

Cold terror coursed through Kendall's body. She stiffened and dropped her notebook and iPad. Images of the last party she'd attended flashed through her mind and her pulse soared. She couldn't breathe.

"Kendall? What's wrong?" Ryan held both her hands and peered into her face.

She couldn't answer. She had to get away—get some air. Her mind raced to remember the techniques her therapist taught her to deal with panic attacks. She turned away and ran out through the school doors. Ryan picked up her things and followed her. When she stopped to breathe, he wrapped his arms around her and held her tight.

"It's okay. You're okay." He repeated the words over and over in a slow, calm voice.

Kendall focused on his solid frame like a fortress around her, on the cold air outside, on the sound of his words. Gradually, she caught her breath and began to relax into the comfort of his arms. "I'm sorry. I—"

"Shh. You don't have anything to be sorry about. You looked really scared. But you're safe. I've got you."

Tears sprang to her eyes, and she cried into his sweatshirt. The bell for the next class rang, but Ryan stroked her back until she stopped. "I feel so stupid."

"What's wrong, Kendall?"

"I don't want to talk about it. I'm really sorry. You're late to class."

"I don't care about class, but I'm worried about you. What can I do?"

"Nothing. Really. I just freaked out. I'm really embarrassed."

"My mom sometimes has panic attacks. Do you think that's what happened to you?"

Kendall looked up at him then. "She does? How does she deal with it?"

"Pretty much like you just did. Tries to focus on breathing and feeling safe, I guess. Once, she went to the hospital because she couldn't breathe. There's medicine for it, but she doesn't want to take it."

"You're really sweet, you know?"

"Don't tell anyone. I have an image to keep up, you know." Half of his mouth curled into a smile and he winked at her. "Are you ready to go back inside?"

Ryan walked her to her locker and then offered to walk her to class. "Unless you'd rather just get out of here. We could drive over to Riverfront Park and just hang out for a while?"

"Ditch class?"

He shrugged. "If you want. If you'd feel better."

She nodded her head. "I'd like that." She put her things in her locker and pulled out her coat. Ryan took her hand and led her out to his truck. "I just have to be back in time to catch the bus home. I wouldn't want my brothers to worry about me."

CHAPTER 24

Dirk sucked the freezing air into his lungs and clutched at the searing pain in his shoulder as he rolled under a dense pine tree for cover. The man in black from the helicopter had shot him! It had happened so fast, Dirk hadn't had time to move before the bullet slammed into his arm. He'd hit the same shoulder the bounty hunter had shot, but this time the shooter did real damage. Dirk desperately needed backup, but he'd lost his sat-phone when he scrambled to escape the shooter. It had fallen from its holster, bounced down a rockslide into a ravine, and sank into the deep snow below. Now, he was injured and couldn't send his coordinates to the ranger station.

His first impulse was to fire back. To take out the son of a bitch who shot him. But if he did that, he'd reveal his position, and one thing he knew was that the man in black was an excellent marksman. He might not survive another bullet. But if McCallum flew away in that chopper, they would likely never find him again, and the stolen American military secrets would go to the highest bidder—to an avowed enemy of the United States of America. Dirk had to stop them somehow. He could not lose McCallum now.

Dirk lay motionless in the icy bed watching, barely able to see the duo through the scope of his M4 across the open meadow from his position behind the low berm of snow. The pain in his shoulder begged him to close his eyes and give in to his desire to sleep, but he blinked hard and shook his head to fight off the urge. He had to keep his focus fixed on McCallum.

It seemed like hours had passed, but his watch confirmed it had only been twenty-five minutes before the black-clad man returned to his matching helicopter and climbed inside. The rotors spooled up, and his shooter was airborne, heading out of the mountain clearing in the direction from which he'd come. Strangely, McCallum stayed behind. Had he given the secrets to the smaller man? If so, now all Dirk could do was arrest him. At least they could find out what he'd sold. The spooks had their ways of forcing him to talk. And once he confessed all, McCallum would spend the rest of his life in a dark, dank cell in Leavenworth, unable to harm anyone ever again.

Dirk had only minutes to tend to his injury before McCallum moved off, or worse, came to look for what his comrade had shot. He felt the back of the wound on his shoulder. There was an exit hole, thank God. Now, to stop the bleeding. With his right hand, he jerked open the pocket on his pack where he kept the first-aid supplies and grabbed a packet of QuickClot gauze. He understood the risks of sealing a gunshot without cleaning it, but at this point he had no choice. He had to keep moving. With any luck, he would apprehend McCallum, use his enemy's communication gear to get the backup he needed, and they could fly him to a hospital before any infection threatened his life. An image of Emory with her beautiful smile and bottle-green eyes floated across his mind. He bit down and jammed the gauze into the front hole in his shoulder.

Dirk did his best not to cry out, but a groan roared from his throat, and he almost passed out. Tears poured from his eyes, and he wiped them away on the arm of his coat. He drew in several quick breaths before mentally preparing himself for a second stab of agony. Panting fast three times, he filled his lungs with air and held it while he forced the fresh clotting material into the backside of his wound. He laid his head back on the icy snow until the dizziness left him. The cold felt good against the heat that coursed through him. He lay there until he caught his breath and his vision cleared. It was time to move.

Checking his scope, Dirk saw McCallum disappear into the edge of the forest that lined the open space. Dirk slung his pack over his right shoulder and forced his legs to stand and run. He stayed within the cover of the trees, which cost him some time, but kept him hidden from the view of his target. Ignoring the throbbing pain in his shoulder, Dirk pressed on deeper into the woods, running when he could. He forced thoughts of his military brethren to the forefront of his mind as motivation to push through the pain and persevere. There was no way he was going to let McCallum sell them out.

Dusk was fast approaching, and both McCallum and Dirk would have to hunker down for the night. It was going to be far more difficult to ignore his injury when he could no longer keep his focus on the chase. He didn't think McCallum knew he was being followed, so when the traitor made camp, Dirk did the same. He strung a tarp between his camp and McCallum's, hiding his small fire and using it as a modicum of shelter. After climbing into his sub-zero sleeping bag, Dirk sat close to the flames and pulled at his shirt that was stuck to the dried blood of his wound.

Though he trembled with cold, sweat dripped from his forehead as he tended to the hole in his shoulder. He cleaned it to the best of his ability before replacing the blood-soaked gauze with fresh QuickClot. There was self-sticking Ace wrap he used for compression before he rested back in the snow, using its chill to relieve the inflammation. He had been shot in the shoulder twice in his life, now, three if he counted the nick from earlier. And it was worse this time. Or maybe it was simply that he was getting older.

Dirk had no way of calling for backup or medical assistance other than with his personal cell phone, which had no coverage up here in the frigid middle of nowhere. He thought of Emory, and his heart ached for her, knowing that he was going to miss their wedding. He had to make it through this so he would have the opportunity to apologize and tell her how deeply he loved her, at least one more time. Dirk's eyelids were heavy, and he dozed for a few minutes. He snapped awake and sat up. With too much ice, he'd kill some of the tissue. He replaced his shirt and pulled the warm sleeping bag up over his head. He was desperate for sleep. Dirk closed his eyes and drifted off on a midnight-blue sea.

POP! The loud noise woke him. POP-POP-POP! Dirk bolted upright.

Gunfire!

CHAPTER 25

Ian slept fitfully. He was overwhelmed with the sense that someone was following him. Rising before dawn, he packed and did his best to cover signs of his camp. It was so much easier to hide your trail in the summer months. Falling snow could be a friend when covering tracks, but old snow left marks, and it was hard to brush over them. After gathering and packing his gear, he hiked to a high point on the mountain from which he could view the entire clearing below and the tree line surrounding it. He tore open two protein bars and leaned back on his pack to watch.

It wasn't long before he saw what he had suspected. The operative had been wrong. He had fired at something, but it was still moving. The flickering of a small flame just inside the trees on the far side of the open space. His instincts were good, but he wasn't happy about what he observed. The "something" the Chinese guy shot had survived and was still on his trail.

Ian wanted to get to Canada as soon as possible. He

was no longer welcome in the arms of the great United States of America, and it was time for him to disappear. But he had to take the time to wait out the man who was hunting him. Anger licked the back of his throat that he had to spend a valuable hour to tend to this crucial task. He swung his rifle up so he could peer through the scope. A silhouette of a man moved in front of the flame. *Sloppy fool.*

Ian moved the crosshairs of his scope, until it marked center mass. He let out half his breath and then squeezed the trigger. POP! The shadow man fell and then rolled, morphing into a larger shape. POP-POP-POP! Ian fired until all movement stopped.

How did his tracker get so close to him without his knowing? He was losing his touch. Definitely time to retire to a deserted beach somewhere in the South Pacific. At least he was on his own now. He should have no more interruptions until he was safely inside Canada.

Ian gathered his pack and struck out, heading north up the glacier.

CHAPTER 26

The muzzle blast gave away McCallum's position on the side of the mountain, but Dirk couldn't see at what he was shooting. It was too risky for the fugitive to hunt game, and besides, Dirk had spotted no deer, elk, or bears. What would cause a professional like McCallum to give up his location like that? Something was off.

Dirk's entire arm throbbed. His hand stung with pins and needles as he shrugged out of his sleeping bag and packed up his gear. The morning air was bitter cold, and an icy wind blew down from the glaciers. His stomach rumbled, but there was no time to eat. He'd grab what he could along the way. He wanted to round the clearing and see for himself what had drawn McCallum's fire, but if he did, he'd lose sight of him.

Continuing to use the forest pines for cover, Dirk jogged through the trees and up the rocky incline toward the location of the gunfire. Each stride jarred his aching shoulder. Before he reached the mountain, he happened upon McCallum's most recent camp. Even though the guy had dumped snow on his fire, it melted, and some of the burned sticks still gave off heat. Dirk was close, and McCallum was becoming careless.

He tracked the traitor all morning. It wasn't hard. The man was no longer bothering to hide his trail. Large, obvious boot prints tromped through the snow, but Dirk was moving slower. He was weak and getting weaker. More than once, he considered stopping altogether, building a shelter and waiting for help to arrive. The thoughts, of course, were the lies of a struggling mind. He reminded himself out loud that no one knew where he was. If he gave up now, he would die of blood loss and exposure. He had to keep going.

Low on energy, he stopped to refuel. His MRE menu was getting sparse. He cut open the sturdy plastic covering of the first meal he pulled from his bag, and dumped out a pack of chili with beans, cheddar cheese spread, cornbread, and a fortified carbohydrate drink powder. He took barely enough time to heat the chili to lukewarm with the flameless ration heater before he gobbled it all down, then he dissolved the lemon-lime mix in water and chugged it. Within minutes he felt like a new man. He drank a packet of hot cocoa for dessert, reveling in a surge of energy as the sugary liquid infused his blood.

With renewed hope and focus, Dirk set out following McCallum's tracks once again. He estimated he'd lost another half hour. With his injury, Dirk had a limited amount of time and go power, and he needed to use them wisely. His pack seemed heavier than before, and he considered dumping some items out of it, but everything he carried was necessary for his survival in this brutal environment except for his meal trash. He hated to leave it in the wilderness. It went against everything he'd learned about leaving no trace, but his bag would weigh less. Not by much, but even a few ounces mattered to him at this point.

Dirk followed McCallum's footprints up the mountain until they stopped at the bottom of a two-hundred-foot rock wall. He looked to the left and right—no prints. He tilted his head up. Sure enough, there was McCallum, scaling the cliff approximately sixty feet up the slick side of granite. With his shoulder in the condition it was, climbing was not an option for Dirk, but McCallum provided him with the solution. He was an easy target hanging up there. The challenge was going to be stopping him without killing him. The FBI wanted him alive. Of course, that might not be possible.

After he took a second to wipe the frost from his eyelashes, he swung his M4 up to his right shoulder and squinted to peer through the scope. Since his left hand was useless, he leveled his gun on the rock and pulled the butt tightly against his right shoulder. He fired.

McCallum cried out. The sound bounced against the rocks and ice. An MRE package clattered down the rock face, followed by Ian's tarp and a first-aid kit. More survival gear rained down around Dirk, and he shuffled sideways to avoid being hit. He must have blasted the guy's pack. After the last item fell to the ground, Dirk looked up to see if McCallum was alive, but he was gone.

"Damn it!" Dirk kicked Ian's compacted sleeping bag,

which flew like a soccer ball into the trees, leaving behind a dull black rectangular device that had been hidden beneath it. McCallum's sat-phone! Dirk lunged for it, hoping it wasn't damaged in the fall. If it was still working, the phone was nothing less than a lifesaver. He gripped it and dialed the number for the FBI's task force. His breath came easier as hope soared. Now he would get the backup and medical care he needed. Sliding to the ground beside the device, he heard, "FBI Field Office, Missoula, how can I help you?"

Dirk went limp with relief as he identified himself. "I need to speak to SAC Reagan immediately."

"Hold please."

While he waited, Dirk pilfered through the other items that had fallen from McCallum's pack, looking for anything he might be able to use. A massive boom shook the ground, and the dirt inches from Dirk's boot exploded. Before a conscious thought crossed his mind, his body instinctively rolled to the side. He scrambled for cover behind a group of boulders at the base of the cliff. More shots followed, pinning him behind the stones. McCallum was fighting back from above.

Dirk had dropped the sat-phone when he took cover, and one of the stray bullets meant for him struck the device. The phone bounced into the air and splintered before dropping to the dirt. It lay shattered in pieces on the ground.

The hope Dirk felt only seconds ago vanished. In that moment, he had become the hunted. McCallum now knew Dirk was tracking him and would do what he had to do to take him out. Dirk had to find better cover—

immediately. The sun was low in the sky, and temperatures were dropping fast. He needed to move.

Dirk pulled a space blanket from his pack. Unfolding it, he tossed the shiny metallic sheet over the boulders to the ground at the base of the granite mountainside. McCallum fired no shots. This was both good and bad. Good, because McCallum was no longer poised to shoot him from above if he moved; bad, because it meant McCallum was on his way down the mountain to make certain Dirk was dead. He scrambled over the rocks, grabbing the blanket but in his rush, left everything else.

His best bet was to find high ground while doing everything he could to cover his tracks. The snow was his ally when he was the one who was tracking, but now that McCallum was looking for him, it was his enemy. Dirk located a climbable Ponderosa pine, but before he went up, he confused his tracks by walking around in circles and heading off in multiple directions. He cut a pine branch to use as a broom to dust over the trail that led to his hiding place. It wasn't perfect, but with the sun going down, he hoped it would be enough.

He struggled to climb as high in the tree as he could with only one hand, scraping his face on the rough bark. His shoulder burned with the effort; the pain in his arm drained him. He wedged his body between two branches and wrapped the space blanket around himself so he wouldn't freeze to death, inadvertently doing McCallum's job for him. Using his teeth, he tore open a protein bar and wolfed it down. There was no time for more. He replaced his rifle magazine with a full one, propped the muzzle on a branch, held the firearm at ready and waited.

Huffing breaths echoed between the trees. Snow crunched. McCallum was somewhere nearby, breathing hard from his descent. Though his body tingled with adrenaline, Dirk held perfectly still and slowed his breath, making no noise at all. McCallum crashed through the woods, following the circling trails Dirk had made. Eventually, McCallum's footfalls stopped. A beam of light bounced across the forest floor. He must have believed Dirk was no longer in the area or he wouldn't have turned on his Mag light, making himself a target.

When McCallum appeared in his rifle sight, Dirk would shoot.

CHAPTER 27

Emory finally got home around eight. The kids had eaten pizza for dinner and had cleaned everything up before she arrived. "Hi gang. Did everything go alright while I was gone?"

Kendall looked up from her phone. "Yep. We did our homework and now we're just chilling watching TV."

"How was school?"

"Fine."

"Boys?" They were glued to their show. Emory clapped her hands. "Hey, boys!" When they turned toward her, she repeated. "How was school?"

"Dumb," Jack refocused on the TV. "But I got to practice at QB!"

"That's great! Congratulations! Joey, how about you?"

"Good." He was already staring at the screen again.

"The TV goes off at 9:00 pm, guys."

"Okay..." they all murmured.

Emory turned on her electric kettle to make a cup of tea. Hopefully, she'd be able to relax. At least a little.

Tomorrow was supposed to be her and Dirk's wedding, but she hadn't heard from him. She called her mom to tell them they would have to postpone their flight.

When Emory and the kids went to bed, she couldn't sleep. She lay still in the dark, letting a wave of crushing worry wash through her. Another comforting cup of tea was the medicine she needed, so she stretched and rolled out of bed. She wrapped her forest-green velour robe around herself and cinched it at the waist before she made her way across the unlit house to the kitchen.

She was eager to see what would turn up after she and Henry had stirred the pot earlier that day. Hopefully McCallum's fellow rats would show themselves with the scurrying she and her young deputy set into action. The FBI itself would track the phone calls Preston made from his office and had promised to have him followed over the next few days.

Emory poured boiling water over the bag of Earl Grey tea. She inhaled the comforting floral aroma and swirled in a spoonful of sugar. While she waited for her drink to steep, she peeked in on the kids. They looked so peaceful while they slept as though they hadn't survived the tragedies that had crashed into their lives.

Back in the living room, she opened her laptop to check on Kovalenko and his Ukrainian mob family. She rolled the bottom corner of her lip in and bit down. Her search showed that every one of them were still safely in prison. That was good, but if they were all in jail, then who sent the strange snap to Kendall? And who tried to run Emory off the road?

She sipped her sweetened tea and curled up on the

couch with her computer, deciding to delve into the man Henry discovered in his search. Colonel Steve Webber—retired from active duty but now working as a military systems consultant to the Pentagon. She studied the photos that Henry had found of the colonel and McCallum together. If they were working together, it explained how McCallum got a hold of the military secrets he wanted to sell. But what was in it for Webber? She took another sip of tea while her brain wrestled with the question.

Emory read through all the articles she could find about the colonel's career while the rest of Billings slept. Webber had what appeared to be a successful life in the Army. But there was one incident when he was the CO of a unit in Afghanistan. A mission went sideways, and speculation was that a CIA analyst sold the unit out to save an insurgent they felt was more important to the US than their own men were. As she read further, she learned McCallum was a member of that unit.

Yawning, she stretched and got up to refill her mug before diving back into the files. Her vision became bleary as she scanned line after line, until a familiar name caused her to stop. She started at the top of the paragraph again and read more slowly. Lieutenant I. McCallum transferred out of that unit after the failed mission. A short time later, he joined the Delta Force via a recommendation from General Warren Pole. The accompanying photo showed the two men shaking hands. *Warren Pole... as in Deputy Director of the FBI Warren Pole?* Goosebumps scattered across Emory's skin. She set her tea down and read the article one more time.

Suddenly, it occurred to her who was behind the man hired to run her off the road. It wasn't the Ukrainians at all. It was her dad's old friend, Warren Pole. Everything became crystal clear. Of course, Pole, Webber, and McCallum were *all* in on this. The whole evil operation made her sick, and it was her job to reveal what she now knew. Emory whispered a quick prayer for Dirk's safety and that he would catch McCallum.

She reached for her phone and dialed Dirk's sat-phone. It was the middle of the night, so it didn't surprise her when her call went to voicemail. Dirk wouldn't have the device on when he was trying to remain invisible, but she was happy to hear his recorded voice, anyway.

Emory began to fill him in on what she had found when the kitchen window exploded, shattering into thousands of shards. As she dropped to the floor, she cut the call and dialed 911. Before the dispatch answered, she crawled to the master bedroom where she opened the gun safe by her bed. She retrieved her Glock, and crouching, she hurried to wake the kids.

She shook Jack. When he woke, she ordered him to take Joey to the basement. "There's a room down there with no windows. It's fortified..."

"Like a safe room?" His dark brown hair stuck out at all angles, and he stared at her wide-eyed.

Emory hated that Jack even knew what a safe room was. She swept her hand across Joey's cheek to wake him. "Yes, sort of. It will do. You boys go down there, now. I'll get Kendall." She ran toward the girl's room. Headlights swept through the living room. A gunman strafed the house with bullets. Kendall screamed and flung open her door. "Kendall! Get down!" Emory yelled. "Stay low and go down to the basement with the boys."

"What about you?" the girl shrieked. She clung to Emory's arm.

Emory peeled her fingers away. "I'll be fine. The police are on the way. Now, please! Go downstairs!"

Tears streaked Kendall's cheeks and her voice trembled. "Where are the cops who are supposed to be watching the house?"

Emory didn't want to think about that. "I don't know yet. Do you have your phone?"

Kendall nodded, fear engulfing her eyes. Emory's heart ached for the girl; she'd been through so much at her young age. "Go downstairs and call Henry." Kendall began to protest, but Emory pushed her toward the basement door, closing it behind her. She returned her phone to her ear. "Hello?"

"Yes, ma'am. This is Billings Police Dispatch. I heard your conversation. We have units on the way."

"Good. This is Chief Deputy US Marshal Emory Grey. The men shooting up my house are professionals. Warn the officers and call in SWAT!" She dropped her phone into her pocket and made her way to Dirk's gun safe to get his rifles ready to defend her house. No one was going to hurt her kids on *her* watch.

She crept to her bedroom window and peered out. Their house was outside of town on property accessed by a dirt road. The shooter's car turned around to make another run. She pushed open the window. Lifting one of Dirk's hunting rifles to her shoulder, she aimed at the driver. The car picked up speed and steered to her side of the road. Emory took a deep inhale and let some of it out as she squeezed the trigger. The windshield shattered, but the gun kicked her shoulder so hard it stole her breath. The car swerved into the split-rail fence.

A second car rounded the corner, skidding on the gravel road. Ignoring the pain in her shoulder from the rifle kick, Emory raised her gun. How many shooters would she have to face?

The truck steered directly toward the house, skidding to a stop in the front yard. It was followed closely by a SWAT vehicle. Officers poured from their tank-like ride and converged on the wrecked car. Henry jumped from the truck and ran toward the house. Trembling, Emory slid to the floor. She rubbed her tender shoulder and waited for him.

"Chief! Emory?" Henry yelled as he rammed open the front door.

Emory got to her feet and went to the living room to meet him. "I'm here. We're okay. The kids are all downstairs."

"You're hurt." He moved toward her.

"No. I just received a swift kick from Dirk's Browning, that's all." She gave him a lopsided grin. "It isn't the Ukrainians this time, but you're never going to believe who's at the bottom of all this."

CHAPTER 28

McCallum never discovered Dirk's brushed-over tracks and eventually gave up and left the area. Ian had probably gone to find a decent place to sleep for the night, but Dirk didn't dare move in case his adversary was somewhere lying in wait.

Temperatures dropped into single digits, making Dirk wish he too could set up a camp with a fire to warm himself. His shoulder screamed in pain every time he moved. Climbing the dense tree had stressed his injury, but getting back down was going to be worse.

Dirk was unaware the first time his eyelids closed, but his head did a lazy-chicken, and he jolted awake when his chin hit his chest. He needed rest, but first he had to make sure he wedged himself in tight enough that he wouldn't fall from his perch when he slept. He shimmied inside his sub-zero sleeping bag and tucked the space blanket around that before finding a web of branches that would hold his weight through the night.

Dirk woke in the predawn light to the solo cry of an

eagle. He was burning up with fever. That meant infection, and that would slow him down, if not stop him completely. He needed medical attention, but with both sat-phones out of commission and his cell out of coverage, and with a dead battery, he would never get the help he required. He shifted, and red-hot pain sliced through his shoulder like a sword. He gasped for breath.

His first priority was to ease himself down to the ground and stabilize his injury the best he could. Using his legs and right arm exclusively, he both climbed and slid out of the tree. It was impossible to descend without hitting his shoulder on several limbs on his way down. Each contact made him dizzy, and he prayed he could get down before he passed out and fell.

His feet finally sank into the snow at the base of the tree, and he collapsed to his knees. Lying back, he cooled his inflamed shoulder and fiery head in the snow as he waited for his vision to clear and to catch his breath. He sucked a lump of snow to soothe his throat, and when he was ready, he retrieved his first-aid kit and braced his mind for the upcoming pain. He wadded up a spare t-shirt and stuffed a handful of cloth into his mouth both to bite on and to cover any sound he might make when he tore the clotted gauze from his wound. He uncovered his shoulder, and taking hold of the bloody clotting material, he yanked hard. Screaming his agony into the cloth buffer, he blacked out for a few seconds.

Even when he regained his wits, his rapid breathing made it hard for him to stay conscious. Blood oozed from the wound, staining the pristine snow. As long as he didn't lose too much, he would actually benefit from the cleaning process. He tore open a packet of alcohol. It wasn't the best way, but in his circumstances, it was the only means he had to kill the bacteria. He squeezed the liquid into the bullet hole and cried out into the wadded cloth again. Sweat poured from his brow as he forced himself to draw air in through his nostrils to calm his breathing. He panted, like a woman in labor.

It took several minutes to recover enough strength to continue. He packed a new set of QuickClot gauze into the wound. After dry-swallowing four ibuprofen tablets to help with the pain and inflammation, he dressed his ravaged shoulder.

The next priority was water and food—in that order. Dirk was losing time, but he'd never make it if he didn't fuel and hydrate his body. He gathered a few sticks and made a small fire to melt enough snow to fill his Camel-bak. He wasn't hungry, which he knew was a danger sign, so he force-fed himself an MRE. This time he ate salty fake eggs and corned beef hash, washing it all down with a powdered energy drink.

The food and water did their magic, and soon Dirk had enough strength to move on. He followed the tracks that McCallum had left the night before when he left the cover of the forest, and they led straight back to the rock wall. Ian had collected the items that had fallen from his pack when Dirk shot it, except for the shattered sat-phone. It remained in pieces on the ground. McCallum had obviously slept at the base of the cliff and had warmed himself with a fire that he didn't bother to cover. He must have re-climbed the cliff in the watery, peach-tinted dawn since there were no other signs of him anywhere.

Dirk let out a gust of frustration. The fastest way up the mountain was to scale the granite face, but that was impossible for him with his useless arm. His only option was to climb the steep mountainside at the side of the rock, bracing himself against the stubborn trees and gorse that grew at the intense angle. He took a deep breath and a long drink before he hiked the half mile to the edge of the rock face to begin his climb.

The summit appeared to be approximately two hundred feet almost straight up. He used his ice axe to pull himself up the mountain. The rope was looped around his waist, and he tied it to trees along the way, to secure his slow progress and keep him from falling. The boots he wore were meant for cold temperatures, not mountain climbing, and he frequently slipped. One foot upward, two back. Not only did his injury slow him down, but he felt every year of his age. Every muscle in his body ached. He was too old for this shit.

That thought led to images of Emory. It was supposed to be their wedding day. Em, he knew, was putting on her brave face, but he also knew she was brokenhearted. How would he ever make it up to her? He wanted to have a family with her—grow old with her—but at this point, he didn't even know if he was going to make it home to her at all. Yet, if there were any way possible, he'd do whatever it took to make it happen.

Hours of agonizing exertion later, he breached the top of the cliff. Pulling himself on top of the mesa, he rolled safely away from the edge and rested, gasping for air. The sun blazed down on him from directly above. It was near noon. As soon as his breathing stabilized, he sat up and pulled two high-calorie protein bars from his pack and gulped them down with what remained of his water. He studied the flat-top and found McCallum's trail. The man clearly didn't believe Dirk was a threat any longer, which might be true. But the fugitive's complacency made Dirk's job a little easier.

He rose to his feet and followed McCallum's boot prints, wondering how far behind the man he was.

CHAPTER 29

Hank drove Emory and the kids to a hotel for the rest of the night. He booked them in for a week under his name so it would be harder to trace. Their house had been torn to shreds, and it would be at least that long before they could go home. Hank recommended they stay in the suite until Dirk got back. He knew his partner would want it that way. Emory finally calmed the children and got them into bed. Kendall had been hysterical, feeling that the attack on their home was all her fault.

He'd made Emory a cup of chamomile tea while she settled the kids in their beds.

"Thank you, Henry. For the tea... and for coming to our rescue."

"Ha! You didn't need rescuing. That scumbag is lucky to be alive."

"Is there any word on his identity? On why he shot up our house?" Emory's voice wobbled, and Hank pulled her in for a hug.

"Not yet. But we'll get to the bottom of this. For now, try to get some rest. I'll call you in the morning."

"Okay." His boss followed him to the door. "Thanks, again."

"Lock every lock on this door."

Emory smiled. "I will. And I have my gun by my bed."

Once Hank was sure he had Dirk's fiancé and his kids safely tucked into their hotel, he drove back to their house. He'd left Evie with Teresa the night before, and it was too early to pick her up, so he returned to see what he could learn from the scene of the crime. The sun was rising as he turned onto the dirt road leading to Dirk's house, and he slid his sunglasses on to ward off the glare.

Bullets had shattered all the front windows. Round holes pocked the façade. It wasn't a pretty sight for Dirk to come home to, but thankfully the Chief's fast actions and excellent shooting had kept their family safe. They could repair the house. Hank wondered about the kids' emotional state, though. They'd been through so much, he hoped they would all be able to heal.

He parked in the driveway and walked along the front of the home, taking in the splintered porch railing and the shredded shutters. The cops called for the car to be towed, but the destroyed split-rails of Dirk's fence lay across the grass like scattered Lincoln Logs. There was crime scene tape still wrapped across the front steps, but the detectives had gathered what they needed and left. Thankfully, there had been no casualties. Even the man in the car that Emory shot was going to be alright. In fact, the hospital would be Hank's next stop. He wanted to talk to the shooter and find out who he was and why he was after Dirk's family.

Hank studied each of the bullet holes. Most were empty, but he found one in a tree to the side of the house that still had a bullet lodged inside. The cops had missed it. He dug it out with his pocketknife. It looked to him like the 5.56x45mm round used in an M4 Carbine. The same rifle he used. The same rifle issued by the US military and most of the police forces. That in itself didn't tell him much, but he filed the information away in his mind.

He made his way to the back of the house, which was untouched by the attack. Crossing the patio, he tried to open the back French doors. They were unlocked, so he went inside. Splinters of glass covered the floor in the kitchen and front bedrooms. Some appliances had sustained damage. But all of it could be replaced. His chest warmed with gratitude, knowing that no one in the house had been hurt.

Glass crunched under his boots as he entered the master bedroom where Emory had positioned herself to fend off the shooter. Dirk's gun safe stood wide open. The investigators had collected his various handguns and rifles for security and as potential evidence. He went to close and lock the door when he heard a noise coming from below. Someone or something was in the basement. Thankfully, Hank carried his own sidearm when he was off duty. He checked the magazine. It was full and he had one in the chamber.

Doing his best to make his own footfalls silent, he crept to the basement door, which was open a crack. The carpeted stairs helped his stealth as he descended into the dark rooms below. At the bottom of the steps, he stilled to listen. A scuffling noise sounded from the back room that Dirk used for his at-home office. Hank held his handgun at low ready and cleared the other rooms and a bathroom as he approached the office door. Holding the firearm in his right hand, he eased the door open with his left.

The door slammed hard against his extended right hand, causing him to lose his grip on his Glock. It clattered to the floor. He dropped to a knee, and rammed his shoulder against the door, forcing it open. The man on the other side expected him to be standing, so when Hank lunged up from his crouched position, he caught his assailant off guard, knocking his gun out of his hands, too. Hank swung his fist, connecting with the intruder's chin. The man fell to the floor like a fifty-pound bag of oats.

Using a lamp cord to tie the man's wrists, Hank checked him for other weapons. He found a Beretta Tomcat strapped in an ankle holster and a three-inch fixed blade in a sheath on his belt. After removing the weapons to a safe distance, Hank picked up his Glock and knelt by the man and slapped his face until he came to.

"I know you. Chief Grey and I were in your office yesterday. Imagine my surprise seeing you here this morning, breaking and entering into a federal officer's home. What are you looking for, Preston?"

The shamed FBI agent stared back with belligerence flashing in his eyes. "I'm searching for clues. Same as you."

"Clues for what?"

The man spat blood from his split lip. "I'd heard there was a break-in at Chief Grey's house, and I wanted to see if the cops missed anything."

"You want me to believe you flew all the way up here from Colorado Springs, in the middle of the night, to investigate after the cops left? How did you hear about the crime so fast?" Hank scoffed. "You must think I'm a complete idiot. Now you have one more chance to tell me the truth."

"Or what?"

Hank stomped on Preston's knee, then aimed his Glock at the same joint. "Or you'll be ordering a prosthetic."

"You'll go to prison for torturing me, and none of your testimony will ever be allowed in court."

"Nah, the whole thing happened in a shootout when I found you robbing the Chief's house. My word against yours. Who do you think has more credibility?"

"I'm not telling you shit."

Hank fired his gun. The bullet grazed the inside of Preston's knee, and the man screamed. The crotch of his pants grew wet, and the room filled with the odor of urine. "I think you will. We know you had a hand in McCallum's escape from federal prison, but you didn't do it on your own. Who else is in on this? I want names, and I want them now."

Preston broke down in tears. "I can't tell you. You might blow off my leg, but you won't kill me. They will."

CHAPTER 30

By early afternoon, the sun was high in the sky, and Ian stopped to refuel. The air was crisp and thin. The altitude made him sleepy, and he longed to fill his lungs with pure oxygen. The edgy feeling crawling on his skin made him certain he was still being followed. He'd been sure he'd taken the guy out, but then he magically reappeared. Whoever the man on his tail was, he had to be a vet—maybe even a special forces operative like him. He was good, that was undeniable. The man's skills and persistence impressed him. Ian had seen blood at the base of the cliff when he had camped there the night before. Clearly his pursuer was injured, and yet he maintained focus on his objective. The fact that it had taken Ian several hours to realize his pursuer was still on his trail confirmed the guy's obvious expertise.

Ian was thankful that he had retrieved the gear that had fallen from his pack when the guy shot at him on his climb. It was pure luck he hadn't been killed, and equal fortune that his computer didn't crash down the rocks along with the other stuff. His sat-phone was dead, but he only had another day or two before he was across the border.

Ian respected his hunter, but it was time to end his opponent before the guy prevented him from getting to Canada. He'd set a trap to catch him. Ian hated the thought of killing a brother-in-arms—at least face-to-face —but he had to do what he had to do. He didn't miss the irony that the secrets he was selling would ultimately end the lives of hundreds, maybe even more, of fellow soldiers. The knowledge prodded his conscience, but he stubbornly brushed the annoying guilt away and replaced it with thoughts of his luxurious future instead. It would all be worth it in the end. It wouldn't be long now.

Finishing his bland food, Ian wadded up a scrap of foil wrapping and left it on the ground. He walked through the snow without covering his tracks, making his trail obvious. There were rocks he could have hopped on to prevent leaving marks, but he chuckled and snapped a thin branch, leaving the broken end hanging. The man hunting him would easily follow his tracks until they vanished leaving his hunter in an open clearing.

Ian would lie in wait nearby, and have him, dead to rights.

CHAPTER 31

Dirk was surprised that McCallum was getting so sloppy, but he was eternally thankful. His body was burning up with fever and weakening by the mile. Dusk crept in, and he craved rest, but it would have to wait. He was close, and it was time to start circling his target—tightening the noose. As the sky darkened, Dirk noticed a small flicker of flames about fifty yards to the northwest. It was almost insulting that McCallum thought so little of him that he shined a light, so to speak, on his exact location. Shivering with chills, Dirk made a wide circle through the trees, slowly closing in on the campsite.

Darkness arrived quickly in the mountains, especially with an overcast sky that hid all light from the moon and stars. Dirk crept to the edge of the tree line surrounding McCallum's minimal camp setup. His target lay close to the warmth of the flame, underneath a small tarp in his subzero sleeping bag. Dirk took short, silent steps toward him planning to sneak up on McCallum and subdue him in his sleep. He wiped the cold sweat from his forehead with the back of his glove. He had to act now, or his fever would soon get the best of him.

An icier chill stilled his muscles and halted his breath when he sensed a whisper of movement behind him. He froze in place, not even allowing himself to blink. Inches from his right ear, he heard a metal click.

"Move and you die."

Dirk remained perfectly still, though his pulse skyrocketed. He ran through his options in his head. His opponent was approximately one foot away, so he could try to spin around and disarm him. Or should he wait out the scenario, hoping for a better opportunity? McCallum hadn't shot him on sight, and there had to be a reason for that. Perhaps the man's intention was something Dirk could use to negotiate for his life.

"Raise your hands above your head." McCallum's voice was as cold and smooth as steel.

"I can't move my left arm. Your friend blew up my shoulder." Dirk complied to his ability, slowly raising his right hand.

McCallum took his Glock from his hand. He pressed the cold muzzle of his gun against the base of Dirk's skull. "Now unclip your rifle."

Dirk let out a pain-filled breath and worked the clasp the best he could with his right hand. His left arm was numb and useless. When the mechanism released, he flung his M4 to the side. It didn't go far, but it didn't matter. He'd never reach it before McCallum put a bullet in his head if he tried.

McCallum patted Dirk's waist but found nothing. Dirk watched him from the corner of his eye as he stepped back about five feet. "Yeah, well you're lucky. I thought he killed you. Who are you, anyway?"

"Dirk Sterling."

"Who do you work for?"

"I'm a Deputy US Marshal."

"Ah... of course. They've sicced the Marshals on me. I shouldn't be surprised."

"No. You probably shouldn't be. There's a whole taskforce out looking for you."

"How many of you are out here in Glacier?"

Dirk gave himself a few seconds to answer. If he admitted he was alone, he would lose any advantage he might have. "There are men from the FBI, Homeland, the Marshals, and even some Forest Rangers working together to bring you in."

McCallum laughed at that. "So why are you out here by yourself, then? The men I shot—were they on your team?"

Dirk remembered the gunfire he'd heard before and wondered, too. If McCallum had gunned someone down, it had to have been those foolish bounty hunters. As far as he knew they were the only other people up there. If professionals were searching the frozen high-country, Dirk would know it because they would have located him first thing. Dirk shrugged in response to the question.

"Not talking, huh?" McCallum nudged Dirk's injured shoulder with the barrel of his gun. "Move."

Dirk cried out at the pain, and a wave of dizziness caused him to sway. His body begged him to lie down in the comfort of the cold white blanket below him. But he ignored the urge and forced his boots forward toward the camp.

"Go sit by the fire." McCallum pushed Dirk again when his feet refused to cooperate.

"How many of you are out here?"

"It's just me." Dirk blinked against the pain throbbing in his arm.

"That's not true. I shot two others down below."

It had to be them. "Those guys were amateur bounty hunters. Pretty sure that adds a couple more murders to your current charges."

Ian laughed. "What's the court going to do? Add more years to my life sentence?"

"It will actually make it a death sentence, I imagine. Here in Montana."

"Ha!" Ian barked out a laugh. "More incentive for me to disappear then, don't you think?"

"You know, it's not too late to turn this around. You can't possibly want to be responsible for the death of hundreds of young soldiers just so you can live in the lap of luxury, can you?"

"Shut up. You don't know anything."

"I know you feel betrayed. And that's something I *do* know about." Dirk desperately tried to keep the conversation going because once it stopped, so would his heartbeat. It was hard to believe that this was how his life would end—in a failed op out in the middle of the mountains. Hikers would find his body next spring, if the wildlife left it alone long enough.

I'm so sorry Em...

"Is that so? What's your story?"

"I'm a former Marine, and as I said, I'm now a deputy US marshal."

"And you want me to believe they sent you up here by yourself?"

"No. There's a whole taskforce dedicated to catching you."

"So where are they?"

"Around."

"Yeah, right. So, you were a Marine, huh? Who betrayed you?"

"It wasn't the Marine Corps. I can tell you that. I'd gladly lay my life down for any one of the men I fought with." Dirk wasn't about to share the intimate details of his life with this traitor.

"I hear you. It's never the soldiers; it's always the brass. They use us as pawns in the quest for rank and glory. They deserve what they're gonna get."

"Sounds like you're the one forgetting that the soldiers and marines are real men with wives and kids, whole families who love and depend on them. You're sacrificing thousands for the hope that you hurt a few. But the men you want revenge on are retired. They might feel bad for a few hours, but that's all. The families of our warriors, however, will be destroyed forever, and none of them ever did anything to you."

"Shut up!" Dirk had struck a sore spot. "My goal isn't to hurt those kids or their families. But I need enough cash to disappear, and this is how I'm going to get it."

McCallum's voice lowered and filled with emotion, maybe even regret. "Look, I'm sorry it has to happen this way, dude. I respect that you were a Marine and you've certainly got the skills and the grit to prove it. But I don't have any other options." Ian was silent for a long moment. "Get up and walk out to the clearing."

CHAPTER 32

Dirk released a long sigh. He struggled to his feet; the snow giving way beneath them. The fever made him lightheaded, and he sucked in a cooling breath trying to clear his mind. He was at his enemy's mercy, and that was a gossamer-thin thread. He prayed he wouldn't pass out. He'd rather face his death head-on than meet it unconsciously.

McCallum holstered his handgun and swung his rifle around from his back to his hands and nudged Dirk with the tip. "Drop the pack."

Dirk lowered his shoulder to let the bag fall, but it got stuck on his coat and remained hanging where it was. McCallum pushed the strap free with the barrel of his M4, and Dirk's supplies fell to the ground. His cell vibrated from within.

McCallum chuckled. "Expecting a call?" He shoved Dirk forward a few steps and picked up the pack. "I'm surprised at you. It's unprofessional to leave your phone on during an op, don't you think?"

Moisture flooded Dirk's eyes at the thought it might be Emory trying to reach him. He was too weak to prevent the tears from dripping down his face. She was so close, and yet he would never hear her voice again. He cleared his throat. "The battery was dead. Maybe the fall jarred some juice into it."

"Let's see who's calling," McCallum jeered as he reached inside the pack to retrieve the phone. He held it up, turning the screen for Dirk to see, and grinned. "Who's the gorgeous blonde?"

Dirk stared at the photo he had chosen for Emory's caller ID through the haze in his eyes, but he said nothing. His throat ached. It was closing in. It hurt to breathe.

"Oops. The call went to your voicemail. Too bad. Seriously, who's the chick?" When Dirk didn't answer a second time, McCallum jabbed the rifle into his left shoulder. Dirk couldn't help but grit his teeth and groan. "I asked you a question."

With nothing to lose, Dirk let himself ease into the comfort of talking about the woman he loved. "She's my fiancée."

"No kidding? You would have been a lucky man... had you not decided to follow me out here. Tell me about her."

"If things would have gone the way I hoped, I would have been home yesterday. Which would have been perfect because today was supposed to be our wedding day."

"Aww, how sweet." McCallum sneered. "What's her name?"

Dirk shook his head. No way was he going to let

Emory's name cross the dirtbag's lips. He changed the subject. "We were planning on adopting three kids as soon as we were married."

"Three?" McCallum's brows crunched together and he smirked.

"Yeah. They're siblings who were in the witness protection program. They lost their parents. No one in the foster care system was willing to take all three, so we decided we would. They've been through hell, and my fiancée and I were determined to keep them together."

"Why were they in witness protection?"

"Long story."

"Oh, I didn't realize you were in a rush." McCallum's retort dripped with sarcasm.

Dirk was exhausted, but he continued talking. "One of the kids was a witness to a mob-killing."

"No way. That sounds like a movie."

"It was a lot more real than any movie. The mobsters found them and killed their dad right in front of them. Their mom was the one who told the mob boss where they were, in return for murdering her husband. She foolishly believed them when they said they'd leave her kids alone, but of course, they lied." Dirk kept talking to delay the inevitable as long as he could. "We got to their house in the middle of a full-on assault. Just in time before any of the kids were seriously hurt. We've been trying to help them heal ever since."

"Sucks they're going to have to cope with your death too, then, huh? It's a sad story, but it doesn't change the ending. Move on out into that open space."

Dirk shuffled forward intentionally moving slower

than McCallum and veered slightly to the left. His captor prodded his good shoulder with the rifle to hurry him along. That was a mistake. The opportunity opened in a blink and adrenaline drenched his system. Dirk swung his right arm around and grabbed the rail adapter right in front of the magazine on McCallum's M4. He jerked the long gun toward himself as he back kicked his captor in the ribs with his boot, forcing him to release the weapon.

McCallum fell backwards and went for his sidearm. Dirk rammed the butt of the rifle into the traitor's face. Blood erupted from his mouth and nose. But the blow didn't knock him out. McCallum's cheekbone had caved in, changing the shape of his features. He spat out a broken tooth in a stream of cursing and blood-stained spittle. McCallum pulled his SIG from its holster.

Dirk dropped the rifle and dove at his enemy. He tackled him to the ground, landing with his good shoulder crashing against the man's chest. The impact knocked the air out of McCallum, temporarily stunning him, which gave Dirk the precious second he needed. He slammed the dirtbag's hand against a rock, forcing the SIG from his grip. The gun bounced to the side. Dirk scrambled for the weapon, his lame shoulder shrieking in agony. He yanked his glove off with his teeth and wrapped his fingers around the gun. Rolling to his back, he fired at his captor.

McCallum had recovered the M4 and held it leveled straight at Dirk's head. Dirk's bullet caught McCallum in his right arm. Screaming, the fugitive dropped his rifle into the snow. Ian fell to his knees. He lunged forward to grasp the M4 with his left hand.

"Don't move, McCallum!" Dirk ordered.

Ignoring the command, McCallum picked up the rifle firing wildly, hitting Dirk in his thigh. The fresh pain nearly blinded him. Dirk forced himself to push past his body's desire to shut down. He lifted the SIG and pulled the trigger. He missed. He searched for something—anything—he could use for cover. There was nothing. Bullets flew like spits of fire from both men's weapons. He had no choice. Dirk continued firing. Unloading his weapon on McCallum until the man stopped shooting back.

Dirk took a round in his chest. His breath rushed from his lungs. The impact felt like he'd been run over by a Mack truck. He couldn't breathe. His awareness hung suspended above him in the cold, starless night. In silence, he watched the scene from above until everything went black.

CHAPTER 33

Bullets found their home twice more in Ian's gut. Fire engulfed him. He fell to the ground, knowing the shots were fatal. Especially out in the middle of an icy national park with no doctors within hundreds of miles. He laid his head on a pillow of snow and felt oddly relieved. He thought of how young and hopeful he'd been when he received his acceptance letter to West Point all those years ago. How proud he had been to accept his commission. What happened to that kid? Why did all of that have to change?

The faces of the men in his unit who had lost their lives floated through his mind—men like Sterling talked about—his brothers-in-arms. Warriors with families back home who were waiting for them to return. He had attended those funerals... saw the faces of their loved ones... grappled with their grief and his suffocating guilt.

Ian had sought justice first. He tried to go through his chain of command but quickly realized his brothers would never receive the honor they were due. The CIA had looked on his men as if they were mere pawns in a global game. Pieces on a board with no faces—with no more value than little chunks of wood they could easily discard.

After that, he threw himself into the Delta unit. He hit enemies of his country hard, hoping to find relief that never came. It was during that time he'd reconnected with some men he knew from his West Point days. Men who had fast-tracked up the ranks. Men like his "buddy" Dale Preston, Steve Webber, and even Warren Pole, who spun a story of vengeance that Ian had bought lock, stock, and barrel.

It became apparent within a couple of years that those men weren't about helping him—they had their own agenda and were only using Ian's expertise to get what they wanted. That's when he stopped doing their bidding. Before he knew it, certain members of the top brass had forced him out of the Army with a dishonorable discharge. An unfair designation that had haunted him ever since. He'd never get a job in security like most of his retired Delta brothers, so he made the opposite choice and became an assassin for hire. There were plenty of jobs, and he was good at it. His conscience was dead—it had been ravaged long ago—and the money for murder was excellent. But killing people for a living was depressing, so when Webber approached him with the idea of finally getting back at the Army and the CIA, he jumped at the chance.

Webber had access to top-secret information that would sell for millions on the black-market. If Ian managed to secure a buyer, he would get eighty percent of the money he brought in. It was an offer he couldn't refuse. With enough cash, he could retire to a tropical island somewhere in the South Pacific and heal from his violent life, in peace.

But before he could make it happen, a hotshot FBI agent spotted him in a bar in LA. What were the chances? The agent arrested him and took him into FBI custody.

Thankfully, his contacts, fueled by their personal greed, devised a plan to help him escape. Deputy Director of the FBI, Warren Pole himself, arranged everything through Preston, who was working at a field office in Colorado. They secured Ian's freedom, and in return all they asked for was a new percentage of the proceeds from the sale of state secrets. They wanted half. Ian jumped at fifty percent of thirty million dollars if it meant he didn't have to spend the rest of his life in prison. Of course, those suckers would have had to have found him to get their share.

Ian blinked his watery eyes open. Tears froze on his eyelashes. He no longer had to run and wouldn't have to live with the guilt of what he had agreed to do to hundreds of young American soldiers. Sterling was right about that. And at least Ian had lost his life to a worthy opponent. Who knew, maybe they'd see each other on the other side.

A gasp of hot air left his lungs. He drew in no more cold air in its place.

Ian McCallum's eyes closed for the last time.

CHAPTER 34

Emory's parents had flown into Billings even though she told them she had to postpone the wedding. At first, it irritated her that they didn't simply roll with the punch, like she'd had to. But her mom insisted they had nonrefundable plane tickets, and that they wanted to come out to visit, anyway. But now, with all the mess that was going on, she was grateful to have them. They came to the hotel room where Emory, Kendall, Jack, and Joey had hunkered down, and they agreed to stay with the kids while she went out.

"I'm meeting Henry at the jail to interview the rogue FBI agent at the heart of this disaster. After that, we're driving out to the house to see what needs to be fixed and get that scheduled. I'll be back for dinner. There's a nice pool downstairs if you all want to go for a swim." She picked up her purse and stepped toward her father. She leaned close to his ear so only he could hear. "Dad, I want you to have Dirk's gun. Just in case. It's fully loaded, and there's an extra magazine in the room's safe. The code is the year I was born."

Her mom went straight to the kids, giving them hugs and reassurance. The general, however, stuffed the weapon into the back of his waistband. He crossed his arms and leaned against the door of the room. "What exactly does Dirk think about all this? Why isn't he here to protect you?"

"Daddy, come on. He's out in the field chasing the fugitive at the crux of this whole fiasco, and I haven't been able to make contact with him for a couple of days. That's why I had to put off our wedding day. Dirk would hate knowing what happened here, but he also trusts that I am capable of taking care of myself and the children."

"Hmph. I'm glad you're leaving me with a handgun, but it wouldn't hurt to have a backup rifle."

Emory rolled her eyes. "That would be overkill." Her dad was a retired Marine Corps general, and he knew how to protect her family if need be. And though she didn't think anything would happen, she felt reassured, none-the-less knowing he was there. "And don't be obvious with the weapon and upset the kids."

"You know me better than that. Now, go get your work done and get back here. I'm more concerned about you running around out in the open."

"The man responsible for shooting up our house is in jail."

"But his partners aren't. It took more than two men to cook up this conspiracy. Dirk is chasing one of them, but there could be others."

Emory was certain her dad was right, but she said

nothing. "I'll be home by dinnertime. If not, I'll call." She hugged and kissed each of the kids and her mother. "I love you guys."

She drove to the jail and met Henry in the lobby. "Good work this morning, Deputy."

"Thanks, Chief. I'm glad none of you were home when Preston showed up."

"I'm sure he knew we weren't there. He was probably staking the place out. So, do we know who the shooter was?"

"Yeah, the cops ID'd him as Jeremy Ford. Guy is ex-military, forced out under circumstances less than honorable. So, a basic dirtbag. Has been jumping from job to job. He told them Preston had hired him to shoot up your house. Claims he was just supposed to strafe the front a couple of times and then take off."

"As a warning?"

"Sounds like it. I guess we pushed Preston's buttons a bit too hard when we visited him at his office."

"No kidding. Let's go find out who he answers to. There's no way that little worm is running this operation on his own."

The BPD receptionist buzzed them in. Henry held the door open for her and followed her through into the interview room. An officer brought Preston in cuffs to the closet-sized space. He made the shamed agent sit and then locked his wrists to the table. "I'll be right outside if you need anything." To Preston the cop growled, "Don't cause any trouble."

Emory leaned forward, holding her hands together on the tabletop. She turned on the recorder, stated the date and the names of those in the room. "What happened to you, Dale? What made you turn into the worthless slug you've become? Not only have you turned against a country that has done nothing but employ and support you, but you tried to have me and three children killed!"

"That's not true, Emory—"

"That's Chief Grey to you, you scum."

Preston sighed. His posture proclaimed his defeat. "I just wanted to scare you. I didn't even know you had kids. When did that happen? Besides, no one was hurt."

"The man you hired was almost killed. He's still in the hospital. And any of us in the house could have been murdered as well. What is wrong with you?"

"If I didn't stop your investigation, my life was on the line, too."

That was the opening she was looking for. "By whom? Who would want you dead?"

Preston shut down and stared at his hands.

"Come on, Dale. You know how this works. You help us, we see if we can help you."

His tone acknowledged his defeat. "You wouldn't want to help me."

Emory glared at him for a long thirty seconds before answering. "You're right. I don't want to help you. But my agency is bigger than my feelings. The US Marshal Service can help you, if you help them. Who else is involved? We know all about McCallum. Dirk is out catching him as we speak. So, who else is involved?"

"What's the offer?"

"I imagine we might accept a plea deal, though I'm

not a federal attorney, so I don't know for certain. But I'm sure you can finagle less jail time if you give us what we need."

"But I'd still have to go to prison?"

"You're a traitor, Dale. You're lucky they don't just shoot you at dawn."

Henry sat forward and stared the man down. "I suggest you give us whatever information you have, cuz otherwise we'll make certain you spend your time in gen-pop and, as you know, cops don't do real well in there. Maybe the next time I see you, you'll have changed your name to Betty."

Preston broke down in tears. "Okay, okay," he blubbered. "But you have to promise to keep me safe in prison. You have to."

Emory relaxed her shoulders. "I can promise that only if you give me names."

"Just one. There is only one name. But it's a big one."

"Okay…"

Preston looked up at her with watery eyes. "The man at the top is Warren Pole, Deputy Director of the FBI."

Emory absorbed the name as though Preston had her punched in the gut. It didn't surprise her because she'd come across his name before, but it made her sick to her stomach to hear the confirmation. How could someone in that position hate his country so much as to sell military secrets to her adversaries?

"We'll need you to put all of this in writing. Include how the organization was set up and all names, dates, and times you remember. You disgust me, Dale Preston. I hope you rot in prison."

Emory pushed her chair back and left Henry to finalize the interview. She stepped into the hall and called the US Marshal's D.C. district office. She spoke to the Chief Deputy there requesting the apprehension and arrest of the Deputy Director of the FBI.

When Henry finally came out of the tiny room, she joined him and they made their way outside. "I can't believe it!"

"Believe it." She stared straight ahead into the overcast day. "Every time I think I've seen the worst of humankind, something like this happens."

"Yeah, people suck." Henry opened her car door for her.

"Do you have time to come with me out to the house? I need to figure out who to call to start working on the repairs. And I need to board up the windows for the time being."

"Sure, but why don't you let me and Jack deal with that? It might be good for him to feel useful. It's a guy thing."

"Really?" Emory wanted to cry but didn't dare. Her phone rang, and she pulled it from her purse. It was a number she didn't recognize. "Hello?"

"Chief Deputy Grey?"

"Yes?"

"My name is Dan Lowry. I'm a Forest Ranger up in Glacier National Park."

"Yes, Dan, Dirk Sterling has mentioned you to me." Ice water sluiced through her body, and her stomach braced for horrible news. "Is everything all right?"

"No, ma'am. I'm sorry to say, Dirk is currently on a

medivac flight headed to Providence Saint Patrick's Hospital in Missoula. Honestly, ma'am, it doesn't look good. If you can get up there right away, I think you should."

Emory's ears rang, and her throat closed over a painful lump inside. She coughed to get her words working. "What... what happened?"

"No one knows for sure. We traced the GPS on Dirk's sat-phone and then followed his tracks from there. We found him and Ian McCallum bleeding in the snow at the top of Mount Crandall. Both men were shot up pretty badly. McCallum was dead when we found them."

Emory blinked and couldn't seem to form any words.

Henry took her phone from her and spoke to the ranger. "We'll be there as soon as we can."

CHAPTER 35

Kendall did her best to put up a brave front, but she was terrified. She would never escape the men who wanted to kill her and that put her brothers, Dirk, and Emory at risk, too. Emory's mom had turned on a funny family movie and bundled everyone up on the couch in extra blankets while she made them pancakes and bacon for breakfast.

Everyone, except for Emory's dad. He pulled a chair over near the door to the suite and sat guard. Kendall appreciated what they were doing, but nothing could chase away the fear that ran up and down her nerves making her skin feel raw. Jack fake-laughed at the show while exchanging glances with her. Last night's attack had him upset, too, but he was worried for her. Joey seemed like himself. She hoped that was true and not a cover like the one she pasted on her face.

Her phone buzzed.

RYAN

> Hey, did ur parents get a call from
> school? I got busted for ditching.

Kendall pressed her phone to her chest and went into the bathroom for privacy. Her thumbs flew over the screen of her cell in response.

> They haven't said anything, yet. We kind
> of had a crazy night. R u in trouble?

Kendall slid down the wall until she sat on the tile floor. Guilt swirled in her stomach. The last thing Emory needed right now was to get a call from the school. Kendall knew she and her brothers were already a burden, and now on the night before what should have been Dirk and Emory's wedding, their house got wrecked. Dirk was on a case and they hadn't heard from him. Emory had gone to find out who was trying to kill them, and now she was going to get a phone call that the girl she was going to adopt was a problem kid on top of everything else.

RYAN

> Not too bad. Just extra chores.

> I'm really sorry. It's my fault. You
> shouldn't have ditched for me.

RYAN

> Not true. Besides, I had fun at the park.
> Did you?

Kendall smiled for the first time that day.

> Yeah, me too. Thanks - you're really sweet.

RYAN

> Want to go on a ride this afternoon? I can pick you up when I'm done with my slave labor.

She had never answered him about going horseback riding with him. How could she explain her life? If everything had gone like it was supposed to, she would have been in Dirk and Emory's wedding that day. If she told Ryan that, she'd have to explain that they were her foster parents and then that opened up another whole set of questions she couldn't answer. And after last night, there was no way her foster grandparents were going to let her out of the hotel suite with a boy no one had met yet.

Her life was full of lies and half-truths. She really liked Ryan and she was already wrecking things by not being honest. If she told him she couldn't go, he'd want a reason. What excuse could she possible give him?

> I wish I could. But when my mom finds out I cut class, I'm going to be grounded for the rest of my life.

Her "mom." Another lie, but one she hoped would change soon.

Someone banged on the bathroom door causing her to jump. "Ken, what are you doing in there? You've been in there forever." Jack hollered. "Other people gotta go too, you know."

"Just a minute! Geeze!" She made a show of flushing

the toilet and then turning on the sink faucet as though she was actually using the bathroom instead of just hiding inside it. Her phone dinged again.

She opened the door and Jack stood blocking her way out. He glanced at her phone and his mouth stretched into a smart-Alec grin. "Talking to your new boyfriend?"

Kendall shifted her gaze to the sitting room behind him to see if anyone had heard him. She did *not* want to have to explain herself to Emory's mom. She whispered, "Shut up, you jerk. I don't have a boyfriend."

Jack tried to snatch her phone, but she whipped it behind her back. "That's not what I hear. Word on the team is that Sorenson has a new squeeze. Imagine my surprise when I heard it was the new chic. That's *you*. Why didn't you tell me you were hanging with the QB? The richest kid in school, by the way."

"Leave me alone." Kendall pushed past him and went into the bedroom where she had pretended to sleep the night before. Closing the door, she checked Ryan's latest text.

RYAN

Maybe I could come over? Tell your parents it was my fault you ditched.

This was so hard. In a normal world, she would be thrilled that a boy who liked her was willing to come to her house to meet her parents and hang out. But there was nothing normal about her life. She couldn't invite him over to the hotel and Dirk's house was all shot up. How would she explain that? And what was Jack talking about Ryan being a rich kid? Ryan said he had a job and had to do chores. None of the rich kids she knew back in Connecticut, including herself, ever had to do chores, let alone have a job.

> Today's not a good day. Maybe next weekend?

RYAN

Okay. Wanna FaceTime tonight?

Kendall didn't know where she might be later, but she answered:

> Sure, if my 'rents don't steal my phone. I'll call you.

RYAN

k 🤍 ttyl

The heart emoji made Kendall's body warm all over, and she hugged her phone. It was clear she wasn't going to be able to hide Ryan from Dirk and Emory forever. Though she should probably tell him she couldn't see him anymore. Dragging him into her messed up life could put him in danger, too. Her heart ached at the thought.

A gentle knock sounded on the door. "Kendall? Sweetheart, everything alrsight?" It was Emory's mom. Her voice softened by her southern accent. "I saved you some pancakes. Are you hungry, hon?"

Kendall cleared her throat and tried to make her voice sound normal. "Just getting dressed. I'll be right out." She wanted the kind woman to like her, and to feel appreciated, but she didn't want to sit with everyone and watch stupid movies. It seemed like she was being fake with all the people she knew, and it was exhausting. She hadn't even been honest with Jack, and they'd always been close.

Her life sucked.

CHAPTER 36

Emory allowed Henry and Teresa to handle all the details. She simply wanted to get to Missoula as fast as she could. Dirk needed her. Needed to know she was there for him. Needed to know he couldn't leave her. Her emotions were so raw she paced the office hoping to ease their intensity.

Henry gripped her shoulders and made her stop.

"Chief, we've got a ride to the hospital on a DEA chopper. They'll be ready by the time we get to the airfield. Where's your coat?"

"Thank you, Henry." She pointed to her office. "It's in there. Let's go." She grabbed her purse and turned toward the door but stopped there. "Wait, what about Evelyn?"

Teresa stood and gripped Emory's hand. "We've got all that covered. I'm keeping Evie with me and Tomas. Your parents are staying at the hotel with your kids. They haven't told them anything more than that Dirk got hurt and is in the hospital in Missoula, and that you and Hank are going up there to be with him. I promise to hold down the fort here. Don't worry. Just go." Tears pooled in the corners of her dark eyes. "And tell that big lug he'd better come back here."

Emory embraced Teresa as a friend. "You know how stubborn he is. He'll be ordering the nurses all around the ward by the time we get there."

"That's right." Hank gave the women a reassuring smile. "So, let's get up there and rescue the hospital staff from his grouchy demeanor."

On the hour flight up to Missoula, Emory picked at her cuticles until they bled. She murmured desperate prayers that the Lord would spare Dirk's life. Numbness pressed in on her as Henry guided her from the helicopter to the car provided for them when they landed. A deputy from the Missoula office drove them to the hospital. Emory stared out at the steel-gray sky as they wound through the city streets. She paid no attention to where they were going.

Before long, Henry helped her out of the car and guided her into the hospital. Dirk's doctor met them in a private room next door to the surgery waiting room. "Deputy Sterling sustained multiple gunshot wounds. One to his left shoulder, one to his right thigh, and a third to his chest."

Emory gasped, and her knees buckled. Henry caught her and helped her into a chair. "What's the prognosis, Doc?" he asked.

The surgeon scooted a third chair over so he could sit facing Emory. "Fortunately, he was wearing body armor when he was shot. It deflected the force of round to his chest which saved his life. However, he has several broken ribs, and a badly bruised sternum. We were successful in his emergency surgery to repair the damage to his leg, but his shoulder had become badly infected, and the bullet tore through the joint. We've stabilized it for now, but he will need shoulder reconstruction surgery as soon as possible. He's currently on IV antibiotics. Now it's a waiting game. I believe the subzero temperatures he endured at the time of the shooting may have saved his life by slowing down the infection from entering his bloodstream."

The doctor's words bounced off her as if she was inside an invisible shell. "Can I see him?"

"He's still in recovery, but yes, as soon as he's awake, he'll be going to ICU. I'm sure having you here will give him the strength he needs to fight the infection. You might like to know he was calling out your name in his delirium before he succumbed to the anesthesia."

Tears flowed unchecked down her cheeks at the doctor's words. "Thank you, Doctor."

"Of course. Wait here, and someone will come to get you as soon as they have Deputy Sterling settled."

Emory's voice floated through his consciousness. He couldn't make out her words, but the sound of them warmed him. Dirk drifted on them as if on clouds. He tried to focus on her syllables, but a fiery pain kept interrupting his thoughts. His entire body seemed to be engulfed in flames. His eyes were closed, but when he attempted to open them, he couldn't. Fear rose in his throat, gagging him. He couldn't breathe. Darkness returned then—the utter relief of sinking into its oblivion.

SOMETIME LATER, Dirk woke to the irritating sound of constant beeping. His head pounded. Had he been out drinking? He opened his eyes a crack. A sliver of light shot pain through his skull. He blinked, and then he saw Emory. She sat slumped over, looking extremely uncomfortable in a chair pulled up to the side of the bed. Wait. This wasn't his bed... or his room. Where the hell was he?

He glanced around and realized he was in a hospital room. He searched his mind to remember what had happened that brought him there. *McCallum!* Where was McCallum?

The beeping increased in speed, and an alarm sounded. A nurse rushed into the room and Emory jerked awake. "What's happening? Is he okay?"

"I think we're waking up," the nurse answered as she checked the monitor and shined a bright penlight into Dirk's already aching eyes.

Emory raced to the other side of his bed and took his hand. "Dirk, thank God. You're awake."

He tried to talk but his throat was sore and dry. "Water."

The nurse nodded. "He can have a few ice chips, to start with."

Emory opened the lid of a plastic carafe on a table next to his bed. She removed two small ice chunks and placed them on his tongue. Nothing had ever felt so good.

He tried to grin, but his face felt stiff. Water dripped out of his mouth and ran down his neck. Emory dabbed at the dribble with a tissue.

"Is this a preview of us in old age?" His throat ached and his voice rasped. "You wiping applesauce off my chin?"

Emory kissed his forehead and touched his lips with the tip of her finger. "I hope so. But only if you stop trying to get yourself killed."

"It's the job, ma'am."

"It's not your job to chase dangerous fugitives into the frozen mountains of Montana by yourself."

"I didn't want to lose him." He drew a breath in and rested before he spoke again. "Dan and the boys were right behind me." He took another break. "Where's McCallum? Did he get away?"

"No." Emory sat on the edge of the bed and held his hand in her lap. "He's dead. His laptop was recovered, and Tech is delving into the device as we speak. We've apprehended all the players and they're in jail."

Dirk sighed with relief. "Good job, Chief."

"You're the one who stopped a traitor from betraying our country. I'm proud of you. Well, honestly, I want to punch you for scaring me like this, but I'm proud of you, too."

"*Shirley*, it's not too late to marry you, is it?"

Emory's green eyes flashed. She placed her hand on his cheek and held his face while she kissed his forehead, his eyes, and his mouth. "You are not allowed to call me Shirley anymore, remember?"

"Why not? Shirley is the name of the hottest woman I

ever met. Did I ever tell you the story of the gorgeous blonde who came on to me at the bar?" He grinned.

"Stop talking, Dirk. You need your rest."

"Okay, but I never agreed not to call you Shirley. After all, you told me that was your name."

Emory tried to look stern, but the love in her eyes told a different story. He wanted to stay with her to reassure her, but his eyelids kept drifting shut.

CHAPTER 37

Once Dirk was stable, his doctors determined he would have to endure shoulder reconstruction surgery. Fortunately, there was an excellent orthopedic surgeon in Missoula who was available to do the operation. When the procedure was over and Dirk was out of recovery, the surgeon told him that everything went well, but that he would have to remain in the hospital for up to three days. More, if his regular doctor felt he needed supervised rest to heal from the combination of bullet wounds, exposure, broken ribs, and his bruised sternum.

Hank had returned home as soon as he knew Dirk was out of the woods, but Emory remained with him. She was on the phone with her mother, asking if her parents could stay at the hotel with the kids until they got home. "If Dad wouldn't mind driving them back and forth from school, I'd feel better about it."

Dirk watched her as she paced the room while talking.

"Thanks, Mom. I don't know what we would have done without you this week. We'll probably be here for a few more days until Dirk's surgeon releases him. I'll keep you posted. Please give our love to the kids. We'll call them later."

The door to Dirk's room swung open. "Hope everyone's decent." The tall, lanky Forest Ranger who had saved Dirk's life sauntered into the room. He nodded to Emory and stood at the foot of Dirk's bed. "You look like you've been drug through hell."

Dirk gave him a wry smile. "I was. I'm told you're the only reason I'm still kicking."

"Nah. That's an overstatement. It wasn't just me."

"Emory, this is Ranger Dan Lowry. Dan, my fiancé and my boss, Chief Deputy Marshal Emory Grey."

"Ma'am, it's good to meet you. And I sure am glad it's with Dirk on this side of the grave. When we found him, we didn't think he'd make it."

Emory reached out and touched Dan's shoulder. "I can't express how grateful I am that you went after him."

Dan shrugged. "We were partners, even if it was temporary. I don't doubt Dirk would have done the same if it were me."

Dirk tried to sit up on his bed and was rewarded with a dagger-like pain stabbing through his ribs, chest, and shoulder. He grimaced and Emory rushed to his side. "Don't try to move on your own," she chastised. "Here's your bed controller." She handed him the device.

He took several breaths before he could adjust the bed and then forced air from his lungs to ask, "What happened out there? How did you end up finding me?"

Dan pulled a second chair to the opposite side of Dirk's bed from where Emory had taken up post. "Well, we found the missing girl. She had fallen into a cavern, which was lucky because she couldn't wander any farther away. She had a few abrasions, was bruised, and cold, but other than that she was okay. Thankfully. Once we got her to the medical tent and to her parents, I went home to get my horse and catch up with you. Imagine my concern when I found my blue roan outside my barn with all his tack still on and no you."

"I tied him to a branch, hoping you'd find him and follow my trail. Guess he pulled loose."

"Yep. He broke the rein and came home. I was putting a new bridle on him so I could come find you, when I got a call from SAC Reagan. He said his office had received a call from you, but that when he picked up the line, you were no longer on the call. He had the call traced and pinpointed its location. He sent a team up to join us, and they picked me up on their way to you.

When we got to the location of the call, we dispersed around the area to search for you. There were tracks all over the place, and it would have been tough to find you, except we had a K9 team from USMS SOG. They led us first to two bodies tumbled together. Both men had been shot and killed by a rifle. We assumed they had come upon McCallum and faced the consequences."

Dirk shook his head sorrowfully. "Those two guys fancied themselves as bounty hunters and were after the reward money for bringing McCallum in. They were way out of their league. I found them only two miles from your cabin. One of them shot at me. Fortunately, the bullet barely grazed my skin. I arrested them and secured them by their fire before calling the Ranger Station to have someone come get them and put them in jail."

"Ah. That makes sense, now. One of the junior rangers went out and finding them bound together, believed them when they told him that the fugitive they were after had tied them up. He let them go." Dan rolled his eyes.

"Well, it cost them their lives." Dirk closed his eyes a minute to recover from the repercussions of his own foolish decision. "I should have stayed with them until back up came, but I didn't want to lose sight of McCallum."

Dan nodded. "From there, we spread out following all the footprints in the snow, many of which led nowhere, until the K9 sniffed out your scent going straight up the mountainside next to the cliff wall. Rather than kill ourselves following your vertical trail, we took the helicopter up to the top. The dog found your scent again and led us to you and McCallum. He was DOA and you were only seconds behind him. Thankfully, we had a medic aboard and he kept you alive until we flew you to the hospital."

"Thanks for coming through. Your expertise and knowledge of the park saved my life."

"It was more the K9, than me. Besides, you'd have done the same for me."

"I would."

The moment drew out and became uncomfortable and Dan rushed ahead. "So, when do you get outta here?"

"Not soon enough," Dirk grumbled.

Emory took ahold of his hand and squeezed. "He has another couple of days resting here, before the doctor will release him to fly home."

"I could rest better at home. Besides, I want to see the kids—let them see for themselves that I'm going to be okay."

"They miss you, too." Emory rose and leaned over him, kissing his forehead. "We can FaceTime them tonight after dinner."

"Well, I better get out of here and let you rest, then. I'm glad you're going to be okay. Stay in touch, will ya?"

"Absolutely. Maybe we'll bring the kids up to the park to camp next summer."

"I'll be your personal guide."

Dan gently shook his hand, nodded at Emory, and left passing Dirk's doctor on his way out the door.

"How are you feeling, Dirk?"

"Like I want to go home."

"Grouchy. That's a good sign." The doctor grinned at Emory who smirked in return. "Okay, let's see how things are going." He checked Dirk's charts and inspected his incisions and wounds. "Good news. You are obviously in excellent shape, and that is playing in your favor. I think one more night in here and, if nothing changes for the worse, we can probably release you tomorrow afternoon. I agree, patients often rest better at home. I'll want to set you up with a doctor I know in Billings for your follow-up care."

"That's great Doc! Thanks."

"But you will have to rest. If you don't, you will end up back in the hospital, is that clear?"

"It's clear to me, Doctor. I'll make sure he behaves." Emory wove her fingers through Dirk's. "Isn't that right?"

He gave her one of his half-smiles but nodded in agreement.

CHAPTER 38

As soon as they arrived home, Emory got Dirk settled in the living room on a recliner. Henry followed them into the house with her and Dirk's belongings.

"Where do you want me to put the firearms?"

"Here, you get Dirk a glass of water, and I'll go lock them in the safe. Thanks, Henry." She took the guns in their cases and locked them safely away in their room. Her mother's voice woo-hoo'd at the front door.

"I hope we didn't get here too soon, but if we didn't bring the kids over, I was afraid they'd walk."

Emory returned to the living room and embraced her mother as the kids surrounded Dirk, plying him with questions, not taking a break to hear the answers.

He laughed and then grimaced. "Hey, take pity on a wounded man, will you? One question at a time. But mine first. Are you guys doing alright? I'm sorry to put you through all this."

Standing tall and proud, Jack answered. "We're good. Uncle Hank and I helped get the house fixed up."

Dirk's dark eyes warmed and he smiled. "Good man. I'm proud of you." He included Kendall and Joey in his grin. "I'm proud of all of you. You guys are the toughest kids I've ever known."

The onslaught of questions flew at Dirk again and Emory laughed. "I need a cup of tea. Can I make you one, Mom?"

"Yes, please!"

"Where's Dad?"

Her mother arched an elegant brow. "Doing a perimeter search. Where else."

"I know you think he's overreacting, but I can't tell you how nice it was to know the kids were safe and sound with the two of you. Dad knows what he's doing."

She and her mom sipped their tea while the kids wore Dirk out with their curiosity and concern. Her dad came in and spoke quietly with Dirk for a few minutes before he approached Emory and her mom. "Time for us to head out, Elaine. Let's let this family get settled. Besides, we have an early flight in the morning." He kissed Emory's forehead. "You've got a good man there, kiddo. I'm glad he's home."

A lump formed in Emory's throat and tears pearled at the corner of her eyes. She could only whisper, "Thanks, Daddy." She walked with her arm around her mother's waist, following her dad to the door where she told them goodbye.

"I'll talk to you next week about plans for rescheduling the ceremony." Her mom kissed her cheek and they left.

Emory returned to the living room and sat on the couch close to Dirk. "Okay, guys, Dirk and I want to talk to you. We've been putting our brains together to come up with a backstory that we can all use. I know you're making friends, and we haven't done a good job of giving you a revised history you can share with them."

Kendall raised her hand before remembering she didn't have to do that at home. Embarrassed, she smiled. "This boy, named Ryan—"

Jack interrupted. "Her *boyfriend!*"

"Shut up, Jack!" Pink stained her cheeks. "He is not! He's just a friend!" Kendall glanced nervously at Dirk who gave her a reassuring smile. "Anyway, he asked where I was from and for some reason I said, Ohio."

Emory reached for a pad of paper and pen that were sitting on the coffee table. "Okay, so you're from Ohio. I think it will be best if you can tell as much truth about yourselves as possible, so other than your true names, what town you're from, and why you are here, you can share yourselves."

Dirk adjusted himself on the chair. "We'll say that your mom and Emory went to college together and that Emory was your godmother. You can explain that your parents were killed in a car accident and that you came to live with her. It's simple and easy to remember. How does that sound?"

Kendall relaxed against the couch. "Good. It's been so weird trying to avoid questions."

"We should have structured this sooner. I apologize for putting you in an awkward situation."

Kendall's phone rang. She looked at the screen and her cheeks flushed again. "Excuse me." She darted to her room and closed the door.

Jack and Joey rolled their eyes dramatically and in unison, said, "It's Ryan, *not* her boyfriend!" Then fell together laughing.

"Who is this Ryan kid?" Dirk's dark brows drew together.

"He's cool. Don't worry." Jack stood and stretched. "He's the varsity QB. Hey, can I have a snack?"

"Of course. Help yourself." Emory glanced at Dirk to see his expression. He was glowering which made her grin to herself.

When Kendall returned, she approached Dirk tentatively. "Um... so... this guy... Ryan? He... um... well, he wants to take me out to dinner. Would that be okay?" She looked at Dirk through her long, dark lashes waiting for his response.

Finally, he raised one of his brows and peered sideways at Emory. She stifled a snicker. He cleared his throat. "Can I have a minute with Emory, alone."

The boys stopped wrestling around on the floor and stared at Kendall. Her eyes widened and she looked like she might cry. Jack got off the floor. "Come on, Ken... Joey... let's go." The boy, who was becoming a man, led his siblings into his bedroom and closed the door.

"Are you okay?" Emory pressed the back of her hand against Dirk's forehead. "You look like you're going to be sick."

"Ha ha. I don't know what to do. I've never had a teenaged girl before. Should we let her go out with the kid?"

Emory shrugged. "I've never done this either, but when my sisters and I wanted to go out on a date, my dad always wanted to meet the boy first. After he scared the crap out of them, if they were brave enough, he usually let us go. At some point we have to trust her."

"She's not even sixteen, yet."

"But she's close. If you want her to wait until then, then that's what we'll tell her."

"Yeah. Maybe he could come to the house to hang out with her and not take her out until she's sixteen. That way I can get a feel for what kind of kid he is."

"Jack likes him and that's a good thing. I agree your plan, but we still need to deal with Kendall ditching school."

"I forgot about that." Dirk closed his eyes and clenched his jaw. "Parenting is so much harder than it looks."

"There's been a lot going on. I talked to her about why she skipped school. I understand her life has been difficult and confusing, but I explained how dangerous that might have been, and that ditching class is unacceptable. But I haven't set a consequence yet. I wanted to talk to you first."

"Should we ground her?"

"I don't know. I'm not sure how effective that would be. She doesn't really go anywhere, as it is. Maybe this time, we just talk to her. It sounds like she had a panic attack and Ryan helped to calm her."

"She left school with *him*? I don't like that."

"They spent the afternoon at the park."

"Well, she's definitely not going out with him until after she turns sixteen."

Emory bit her lips together to hide her smile. "I agree. Let's tell Kendall." Emory went to the boy's room and tapped on the door. "You guys can come out, now."

They filed out of the room like they were on death row. The boys went out back to play. Kendall stood before Dirk and he explained the plan they had come up with. "We want to be understanding, Kendall, but if you cut class again, we'll ground you for a month."

"Okay." Her face was filled with regret. "I'm sorry. I know it was wrong." Kendall looked down at her feet and then back up at them. "So, should I ask Ryan to come for dinner tonight?"

Startled, Dirk looked at Emory. She'd never seen her usually self-assured and confident fiancé so off balance before. Taken out at the knees by a teenaged girl. "How about we wait until tomorrow night since Dirk just got home. Let's give him a night's rest, okay?"

"Okay! Thanks!" Kendall, clutching her phone began texting as she hurried to her room.

CHAPTER 39

During the following week, Kendall invited Ryan over for dinner, but she wasn't the first to break the seal. Joey frequently had Tomas over. But that was a little different because his mom worked with Dirk and Emory. Jack had had a couple of football friends over after practice. They stayed for dinner and hung out for a while afterward. His friends didn't ask questions, though. They just made stupid boy jokes and ate tons of food.

Saturday was her turn. Ryan was coming for dinner. Kendall wasn't nervous about him meeting Emory, because even if she didn't like him, Emory would be polite. Dirk on the other hand, was a loose cannon. He was overly protective and had taken to scowling every time Kendall mentioned Ryan's name. Ryan was a really great guy, but she didn't know if he—or any other boy in the world—would live up to Dirk's expectations.

She had changed clothes three times. Nothing looked good. What did a girl wear when her boyfriend came to dinner. Obviously, she couldn't wear anything that Dirk thought was too short or too low cut, but she wanted to look cute for Ryan. She shimmied out of her plaid miniskirt and tossed it on her overflowing chair. Groaning with frustration, she dug around in her closet to find her floral boho skirt, which was longer. She paired it with a white lacy camisole but wore a jean jacket over that for Dirk's sake. She slid her feet into black chunky, ankle-high platform-boots and after checking out her look in the mirror, moved on to her hair.

Far before she felt ready, the doorbell rang. Emory said she'd get it, but Dirk overrode her. "Nope, I'll get it." Kendall strained to hear what happened next. The door made the swiffing noise it did when opened, but Dirk said nothing. Kendall's heart pounded with anticipation and worry.

"Hi." Ryan's deep voice rang out. "You must be Deputy Marshal Sterling. I'm Ryan Sorenson—Kendall's friend. It's nice to meet you."

Kendall peeked out from her bedroom to see Ryan hold his hand out toward Dirk. Her foster dad didn't take Ryan's hand right away, but made him stand there uncomfortably for a prolonged minute. Maybe she should hurry out and rescue him.

Dirk finally gripped Ryan's hand and shook it hard, but Ryan withstood the pressure and kept his eyes steadily on Dirk's. "Come on in." Dirk opened the door wider and allowed Ryan to pass.

Emory went to him with a welcoming smile on her face. She held out both hands and took Ryan's in hers. "Hi Ryan, I'm Emory. We're so pleased you could come for dinner. Kendall will be right out. Can I get you something to drink?"

"No, thank you, Chief Grey. I'll wait for dinner."

"Alright, why don't you have a seat? And you can call me Emory."

Ryan chuckled. "Not if my mama has anything to do with it." He sat on the chair Emory had motioned him to.

"Ah, old fashioned manners. You don't see much of those these days." Emory glanced at Dirk and standing behind Ryan, he rolled his eyes.

Kendall quickly applied lip gloss and hurried out of her room. "Hi, Ryan."

The young man stood when she entered the room. "Hi." His cheeks mottled with red. "You look really pretty." He glanced at Dirk and amended his statement. "I mean nice."

"Thanks. Do you want something to drink, like a Coke?"

"Sure, if you're having one."

Kendall grabbed two cans from the fridge and joined Ryan and her foster parents in the living room. Joey bolted from his room and sat on the floor watching everyone. "Hi! I'm Joey."

"Hey." Ryan bumped fists with him, even though her littlest brother was just a kid. Joey grinned wide, showing his two adult front teeth, which were still too big for his mouth.

"Dinner is just about ready," Emory said. "Joey, will you please call Jack in from the backyard? And then you two need to get washed up. Kendall, will you help me in the kitchen?"

Kendall panicked. She didn't want to leave poor Ryan alone with Dirk. He might scare her new boyfriend off, altogether. But she followed Emory into the kitchen. "Do you think Dirk will eat Ryan alive?" she whispered as they pulled a salad and fruit from the refrigerator.

Emory smiled at her. "Ryan seems like a confident young man who has been raised well. I think he'll do just fine."

Kendall glanced nervously back at them. Dirk was showing Ryan his gun! She dropped the salad bowl on the counter and rushed to the living room, catching their conversation.

Dirk popped the magazine out of his Glock checked the chamber and then handed the empty firearm to Ryan.

"Yeah, my dad has a handgun similar to this, but mostly we shoot rifles out on the ranch."

"What do you shoot?"

"Coyotes, mostly. But we hunt every year too."

"Where's your dad's ranch?"

Ryan took a beat to answer. "It's the Bar XW, north of Billings."

"Your dad owns the XW? That's the biggest ranch around here."

"Yes, sir." Ryan adjusted his seat.

"I've met your dad. He's a good man. He allowed us to cross his property when we were tracking a fugitive a couple of years back."

"Yes, sir. He mentioned that."

"Well," Dirk gave Ryan one of his half-smiles. Kendall had only seen the man smile fully twice since she'd known him. Once when the social workers agreed to let him be their guardian and the day Emory said she'd marry him. "You'll have to tell him I said, hello."

"He told me to tell you you're welcome to come hunting with him next fall, if you can pull a tag."

"I might just take him up on that. In fact, I just got a new hunting rifle. Let me show you." Dirk stood and Ryan followed him into the master bedroom where Dirk kept his gun safe.

Kendall spun around to look at Emory with all the horror she was feeling as she watched Dirk commandeer her boyfriend. "Seriously?"

Emory's laugh was soft. "Don't worry. This is a good thing. Much better than Dirk glaring at, and grilling Ryan all night long. Let them talk about guns and hunting. After dinner, I'll distract Dirk and you can have some time with Ryan."

"This is so weird!"

"Help me put the food on the table and then call everyone for dinner. And, Kendall, Dirk will relax now that he's shown Ryan his firearms. It's the implied threat he wants him to see. My dad was even worse when I started dating. He would clean his rifle in the living room when I had boys come over and say things like, '*I have plenty of untraceable guns, just like this, and we live on five acres with a tractor. My daughter better never come home crying. Do we understand each other?*'"

Kendall giggled. "That *is* worse! After spending that time in the hotel with the general, I can imagine him doing that. I bet you wanted to die!"

"I was mortified. But when I got older, I realized he

just wanted to protect me. He behaved the same way when he met Dirk, and we're in our forties!" Emory slid her arm around Kendall's shoulders. "It's good to have a dad who loves you and wants to protect you."

"I guess." Kendall tried to sound skeptical, but she knew her smile gave her away.

CHAPTER 40

irk finally got the doctor's approval to return to work—office work only—and he sat at his computer, painstakingly typing with one hand. The office phone rang and Teresa answered it.

"Dirk, SAC Reagan from the Billings FBI field office is on line one, for you."

He pushed the button next to the flashing red light and lifted the receiver. "Sterling here."

"Yes, Deputy Sterling. This is Agent Reagan." Dirk noted he'd humbled his title from the day they first met. "I'm calling to thank you for your work on the McCallum case. You did a remarkable job sticking with him when you could have, understandably, given up to save your own skin. Well done, Deputy."

"Thank you, sir."

"I wanted to see how you're feeling. I know you have a rough recovery ahead of you. Glad to see you're back at work. Do the doctors think you'll be able to return to full duty?"

"I'm doing as well as one can expect and my PT says as long as I do what I'm told, I will be right as rain in another six months. Listen, I wonder if you can fill in a few blanks for me?"

"I'll do what I can."

"I've been wondering what exactly happened up on top of the ridge where you found McCallum and me. I remember we both fired our weapons at the same time. I felt the impact in my chest and honestly, I thought I was done for."

"You almost were. Fortunately, one of the men on the FBI team was a medic. He started CPR as soon as they found you. McCallum, as you know, was already dead when they got there. The team lead called Flight For Life, and they rushed you to the hospital. You probably know the rest from there."

"Yeah. What did you find out about the bounty hunters?"

"A couple of guys who thought they were better than they were. One left behind a young wife and a kid. The other was single. Sad situation, that's for sure."

Dirk swallowed hard. He couldn't help but feel guilt over their deaths. "Did you ever recover the information McCallum wanted to sell?"

"We're still working on that. The team recovered his laptop. It was locked down extremely well, but our tech guys are better. They'll be pulling information from McCallum's computer for a long time."

"And what about the guy in the black helicopter who shot me in my shoulder? Did you ever find him?"

"Unfortunately, no. We're assuming the pilot kept the

aircraft below the radar, flying to and from Canada. You reported you thought the man was of Chinese descent, but that doesn't prove he was working for China. We're still looking for connections to prove that. I'll keep you posted if we find any more information during our investigation."

"Thank you. I'd appreciate it. I don't like the feeling that I've left things unfinished."

"I hear you. We'll be working on this case for a long time, I think. Thanks to Chief Grey's investigation, we've arrested Dale Preston and Steve Webber. Warren Pole will be a harder fish to land, but we won't let go until we know everything there is to know."

"Good."

"I hear you have a wedding coming up?"

"Yes, sir."

"Well, let me be the first to offer you and Emory congratulations."

irk's left arm was still in a sling, so he was forced to allow Hank to tie his bowtie. "Emory always said she didn't want a winter wedding."

"Yeah, well, I think she'd marry you in a blizzard at this point. You really gave her a scare, you know."

"I know. Honestly, Hank, I didn't think I was going to make it out of there. Once I lost comms, I figured I was done for." Dirk looked in the mirror and straightened the white bow of his tuxedo. "It'll be a while before I can come back to work." He made a fist with his left hand. It was going to take forever to regain the strength he'd lost in his arm.

"That's what I hear. The chief says it might be a full year before you can return to field work."

"Yeah, which sucks. I guess the infection really did some damage."

"That and cramming the bullet hole multiple times with QuickClot. That stuff is designed to get you from the battlefield to the medical tent, not as a bandage for several days."

"I didn't have many options." Hank helped him on with his tux jacket, which he wore on his right arm with the left arm empty. "Guess I'll have to be an at-home dad for a while. Once I get my arm out of this sling, you ought to leave Evie with me during workdays."

"What—you think you're suddenly Mr. Mom? No way! I don't want her having to eat weenies and beans for every meal and watching Die Hard all day." Hank laughed and shoved Dirk's good shoulder playfully before he grew serious. "You ready for today, old man?"

"Hey kid, I'm more ready to marry Emory than ever. A year ago, I never would have guessed that my life would turn out like this. I was sure I didn't ever want to get married again, let alone have kids. Now look at me." Dirk grinned. He'd never been happier. "Ready to go?"

"Let's do it."

Dirk and Hank found Jack and Joey waiting for them in a room off to the side of the sanctuary. They all wore matching tuxedos except that Hank's and the boy's ties were black and Dirk's was white. They checked each other's ties and straightened their boutonnieres. Dirk shook hands with the boys and clapped them on their shoulders. "Thanks for agreeing to stand up with me, fellas. It means a lot to have you at the altar with us today."

Jack raised his chin, stood a little straighter. Joey beamed. The guys made their way together to the front of the church and waited, along with the congregation, for Emory. Nerves swirled in Dirk's stomach, though he didn't know why. He'd never been more certain of a decision in his entire life.

The music began to play, and Dirk watched the door intently. An usher, one of Emory's friends from the Tech department, escorted Elaine Grey down the aisle and helped her to sit in her front-row seat. She smiled at him, and he winked at her in return. Tomas, and Laurie's son Caleb, were the next to tromp down the aisle, gripping little pillows in their fists that had the wedding rings tied to them. Dirk hoped they were tightly secured.

Kendall walked slowly behind them carrying little Evelyn. They both wore emerald-green dresses. Kendall helped Evie toss white rose petals on the aisle. When they reached the front, Kendall passed Evie to Elaine and then walked to her spot in the front, across from Dirk. She smiled at the football player in the third pew she'd been seeing, whom Emory had allowed her to invite.

Dirk still wasn't sure about her dating the kid. Ryan was polite and all, and seemed to have good manners. He liked that Ryan had been raised on a ranch. He had a solid work ethic and old-fashioned values, but Dirk would keep an eye on him, anyway. He was certain no one would ever be good enough for Kendall.

The background story they came up with for the kids to share seemed to hold water with their friends. Dirk felt bad that their lives were so difficult, but at least they had each other and a bright future together.

Laurie was the next to enter the room. Her long dark curls were pinned up with a few tendrils hanging down. She wore the same color as Kendall, but it was cut in a different style. By the time Teresa made her way down between the rows of guests, Dirk was antsy. The music changed, and he bit down on his lower lip.

Emory appeared like an angel escorted by her father in his full military mess-dress uniform. General Grey's features were stoic—Dirk expected nothing less. But Emory was a vision in white. She wore her hair up, adorned with tiny white flowers. He couldn't take his eyes off her. He couldn't breathe. Their eyes met and locked. Everyone else disappeared. Her father kissed her and handed her over to him. Emory gave her bouquet to Teresa and took his right hand in both of hers.

Dirk was certain he had said vows and had heard vows, but all he could remember was looking into Emory's eyes. Eyes the rich green color of her brides-maid's dresses. He slid her wedding band onto her finger, and she gently slid his onto the hand resting in the sling. He remembered kissing his bride and hearing Hank whistle. Then it was over. She was finally, really, and truly, his.

At the reception, Dirk and Emory received toasts and chatted with old friends. Laurie brought her new boyfriend, Blake Kennedy, and Ceylon Rahip was there with her fiancé, a Scotsman named Ewen Graham. Hank and Evie sat with them, and trying to decipher Ceylon's Turkish accent and Ewen's Highland brogue became a game at their table for the evening. The newlyweds pulled up two chairs and joined the table for a visit.

Dirk was pleased to see Laurie looking so happy. "I hear your child-care certification came through."

"Yes," Laurie beamed at Hank. "And I *love* watching Evie. She's such a good little thing." Blake slid his arm around her and gave her a squeeze. She smiled as he kissed her cheek.

Ceylon placed her hand on Hank's arm. "How are things going with your ex-wife? I just finished my psych rotation and learned a great deal about bi-polar and schizophrenia disorders. You know you can always call me if you want to talk things out."

Hank released a sigh. "Thanks Cey. Amy's mom told me that she did well while she was in the hospital, but when they released her, she went back to the same patterns. All I can do is hope she figures it all out."

Ceylon nodded sadly. "You can't make her take care of herself. Hopefully, she will come to the decision to do so on her own."

Dirk's friend and co-worker, Caitlyn Reed and her husband Colt Branson, were there with their son Jace, and of course, she wanted to talk shop as soon as the boys all ran off together to slide on their knees across the dance floor.

"So, I followed the story of the moles in the FBI and their connection to the disgruntled Ian McCallum, but what about the mysterious Snapchat sent to Kendall? Did you ever learn who that was?"

Emory accepted a glass of champagne from a passing waiter. "Yes. The tech team was able to trace the snap. It did come from Kendall's old boyfriend. We haven't told her that because it still isn't safe for them to be in contact with one another. We're standing on the WITSEC safety rule of absolutely no contact with their past. I simply explained that the tech guys determined the snap to be unharmful and she seemed relieved." She turned her gaze to the dance floor and smiled when she saw Kendall dancing with Ryan. "Besides, it might be an issue that goes away on its own, anyway."

"So, now that you've got your man at home taking care of the cooking and cleaning," Caitlyn winked at Dirk, "you'll probably need an extra pair of hands in the office?"

Emory laughed. "If you're hinting at a job offer, you already know it's yours. But my counterpart down in Cody, your Chief Deputy, doesn't really want to let you go. He's slow in getting the paperwork back to me. Besides, don't we need to wait until your little one is born?" Emory beamed at Caitlyn's baby bump. "How long will you be on maternity leave?"

"Sorry about my boss. I'll call him and light a fire under his butt. I'll do my best to make sure the documents are on your desk by the time you get home. I'm still working, doing whatever I can from my computer at home, and I plan to do the same thing when the baby is born until my six weeks are over. Then, it's back to work for me and Renegade." Caitlyn glanced at Colt, but he kept his expression neutral. She changed the subject. "Where are you guys going on your honeymoon?"

Dirk chuckled. "Like I'd tell any of you hooligans where I'm taking my bride. I don't trust any of you, except maybe Colt, not to show up and crash the party."

Colt swallowed a swig of beer. "Don't worry, Dirk. I'll make sure my wife stays home even if I have to tie her to a chair."

Dirk laughed at the smoldering look Caitlyn shot Colt. "Don't bite off more than you can chew, Branson."

Dirk took Emory's hand and kissed it. Her sparkling green eyes met his, and she smiled. He'd never dreamed life could be so good.

~ THE END ~

THANK YOU FOR READING **PURSUIT.** I hope you enjoyed some thrilling adventures with Dirk Sterling!

IF YOU LOVED READING the Dirk Sterling thrillers, be sure to check out my **Tin Star K9 Thriller Series** where Dirk first shows up on the scene in, MAVERICK the second book of that series.

I WOULD BE MOST HONORED **if you would please take a moment to write a quick review.**

Review PURSUIT

Thank you so much!

***

The Adventure Continues!

**JODI BURNETT'S
TIN STAR K9 SERIES**

RENEGADE
Book 1

Small Town Thriller!

Caitlyn Reed and her dog, Renegade, are thrown into the midst of murder and intrigue when they discover a dead body while on a trail ride in the black hills of Wyoming. The local sheriff is hell bent on a conviction, and Caitlyn's brother, Dylan, is in his crosshairs. Desperate to prove his innocence, Caitlyn turns to Deputy Colt Branson for help, but she must grapple with their rocky romantic past to gain his aid.

As Caitlyn and Renegade pursue the killer, the investigation catapults their lives in a dangerous new direction, one with mysterious strangers, convoluted clues, and deadly violence. In a whip-cracking turn of events, Caitlyn finds herself under suspicion. When all the chips fall, Caitlyn uncovers shocking evidence that rocks their small-town community to its core.

If you like twist and turn plot lines woven with danger, mystery and suspense, you will love Renegade — Book 1 of the Tin Star K9 Series.

Chapter 1

The inky blackness of the cool spring night soothed Caitlyn's frustration. Relief at having somewhere else to go reaffirmed her decision to move out. The fact that her brother, Dylan, would probably never forgive her was his problem. She absently stroked the furry head resting in her lap as she drove down the forest highway toward Moose Creek. Renegade, her German Shepherd-Malinois mix, slept stretched over the bench seat of her truck, using her leg as a pillow. Caitlyn and Renegade had been together for almost two years now, and she couldn't imagine her life without his company.

Wispy fog rose from the river fifty-feet below to her right, drifting across the highway, permeating the night with a spooky atmosphere. The winding mountain road worked against her like a hypnotist's watch, mesmerizing her toward sleep. She fisted her fingers and ground them into her dry and gritty eyes. Caitlyn cracked open her window to get some fresh air, then reached over Renegade to change the radio station to something more upbeat. She'd barely glanced away from the road, but when she looked up again, high-beam headlights glared into the cab, careening toward her from the black abyss on her left. Caitlyn's brain scrambled to make sense of the direction from which the impending collision came as she instinctively slammed on her brakes. The rear end of her truck fish-tailed and skidded toward the edge of the steep embankment that plunged to the river fifty feet below. One of her back wheels dropped off the soft shoulder, causing a sudden jerk that threw Renegade into the dashboard. He yelped and fell onto the floorboard.

One second before impact, tires screeched and the car racing toward her swerved, barely missing a direct broadside crash, though still clipping her front end. The sick sound of crumpling metal echoed through the cab, and her truck lurched perilously toward the cliff's edge.

Caitlyn stood on her brakes, praying her backend wouldn't slide off, tumbling hood over tailgate to the bottom of the ravine. Never slowing, the smaller vehicle sped away into the night, leaving them to their fate. Caitlyn flipped her pickup into four-wheel drive and sucking in a deep breath, braved shifting her foot from brake to gas. In that heartbeat, the truck bed dropped as the second tire skidded over the edge. She floored the gas, the engine roared, and rocky gravel riddled the underside of her rig.

With a growling surge, the truck fought the battle against gravity until Caitlyn barreled onto solid ground. Once safely on the pavement, she jammed the pickup into park. "Ren? Are you okay?"

Her dog climbed onto the seat and licked her face. Caitlyn hugged him tight and held on, trembling as her pulse steadied and the adrenaline flooding her system receded. She turned the cab light on to check on Renegade. Her hands ran over his bones and belly, searching for lumps and bruises until she was confident he wasn't injured. "Where the hell did that car come from?" Ren answered with another long swipe of his tongue. "That idiot could have killed us!"

Caitlyn rummaged in the glove box for her flashlight. She clicked on her hazard lights and opened her door. It was too dark to see skid marks on the pavement, but the lingering smell of burning rubber assured her they were there. She and Renegade crossed the barren highway. Caitlyn flashed her beam into the foliage on the moun-tainside of the street. Her light panned across a rugged, forest-service entry road. "It was probably just some kids who were up on the mountain drinking and hooking up." She shivered at the knowledge of how close they'd come to slipping off the highway and tumbling down the rocky cliff to the rushing waters below.

Having made sense of where the car came from, Caitlyn and her dog returned to the truck. She shined the light on the dented front bumper. The car smashed her signal light too, but it could have been a lot worse. She opened the door and told Renegade to load up. Once inside, she locked the doors and sat back against her seat, still shaking from the experience. Caitlyn considered calling the sheriff, but there was nothing to tell. Yes, it was a hit and run, but she had only seen headlights and taillights. She couldn't describe the vehicle at all. And besides, this late at night she'd end up having to talk to Colt, and that was something she wanted to avoid at all costs.

Find out what happens next! Get your copy of RENE-GADE, now!

ALSO BY JODI BURNETT

For all book formats

Go to Jodi-Burnett.com

Flint River Series

Run For The Hills

Hidden In The Hills

Danger In The Hills

A Flint River Christmas (Free Epilogue)

A Flint River Cookbook (Free Book)

FBI-K9 Thriller Series

Baxter K9 Hero (Free Prequel)

Avenging Adam

Body Count

Concealed Cargo

Mile High Mayhem

Tin Star K9 Series

RENEGADE

MAVERICK

CARNIVAL (Novella)

MARSHAL

JUSTICE

BLOODLINE

TRIFECTA

QUALIFIED (Novella)

TRIALS

SPEC OPS

DETONATE

US Marshal Dirk Sterling Trilogy

FORGED (Free Prequel)

EXTRACTION

CORRUPTION

REDEMPTION

WITSEC

PURSUIT

ACKNOWLEDGMENTS

Thank you, Lord, for my imagination, for the gift of story, and the strength to finish this book. To my editor, Kae Krueger, thank you for your incredible insight, wisdom, and dedication to making this story the best it can be. To my advance reader team, thank you for your support and willingness to read early and for your support. To my incredibly supportive husband and family, and most of all, to my readers—thank you for trusting me with your time, for stepping into these stories, and for making it possible for me to do what I love.

ABOUT THE AUTHOR

Jodi Burnett is a Colorado native and a mountain girl at heart. She loves writing Mystery and Suspense Thrillers from her home in the Rocky Mountains, where she lives with her husband and her Rottweilers. There she dotes on her horses, complains about her cows, and writes to create a home for her nefarious imaginings. Burnett is a member of Novelists, Inc. and Sisters in Crime. DETONATE is her 20th book along with 5 series companion novellas.